REFLECTIONS

OF A FACE THAT LAUGHS
WITH A HEART THAT BLEEDS

K.R.G. NAIR

ISBN 978-1-956696-89-9 (paperback)
ISBN 978-1-956696-90-5 (digital)

Rushmore Press LLC
1 800 460 9188
www.rushmorepress.com

Printed in the United States of America

REFLECTIONS OF A FACE THAT LAUGHS
WITH A HEART THAT BLEEDS

K.R.G. Nair

Twenty-nine pieces consisting mainly of short stories split into three parts - Frivolity, Digging in and Churning- and based mostly on day-to-day incidents mainly in Delhi and partly in Melbourne giving a vivid picture of India in transition humorously told.

DEDICATION

Dedicated to my son-in-law John and daughter-in-law Meena

Contents

CHURNINGS

FRIVOLITY

1

The Sound of Music

For a family man who had also always kept pets, there is nothing more terrible than having to spend a few days in the family home sans any other living being. I was in this unenviable predicament recently. The rest of my family had to rush off to some place for a few days. On top of it, we had recently lost our pet dog and had not completed yet the process of adopting a new pet.

At the back of my mind, there lurked a genuine fear therefore that I may not be able to survive this period of solitary confinement. To make matters even worse, the monsoon was in full swing. It was raining cats and dogs, ruling out my seeking some solace at least in the company of neighbors. Two days somehow passed and I found, to my surprise, that I was still alive. But I had all along this strange premonition that this seeming tranquility could not last. And it did not.

On the third day, in the morning, I was trying my best to do at least minimal justice to the breakfast that I had laid on the table in front of me. This was most unlike my usual self. Being a health freak, I used to go out of my way to make breakfast my heaviest and best meal. But in striking contrast, I did not feel like touching even a tiny morsel that day. It is true that the bitterness of solitude hung heavily on me on the earlier mornings too. But somehow I managed to make cold practical reason prevail over warm human emotion and could make at least excuses of breakfasts the first two mornings. But then there were limits to patience and these had already been reached by the morning of the third day. I could no longer stand the empty chairs all around the table staring at me. I also badly missed my canine and feline fellow-beings keeping me company on the floor, eagerly waiting to have the share that I would give them after I finished. I did not know what to do and was indeed at my wit's end. It was as if loneliness had started entering even my soul. The inviting aroma of my favorite dish and the unwillingness of a 'stupid' and affectionate soul to have food all alone without sharing it, were having a real tug-of-war. In this, the latter was gaining the upper hand. I was convinced that it was a matter of time before my continued existence with eerie silence all round would make me go off my rocker.

I began experiencing something rather strange. It appeared to me that there were some sounds emanating from somewhere in the room. I knew for certain that there was not a soul in the house and was, hence, a little puzzled. This was all the more so because I had not kept the TV on either. I wondered whether a rodent or some animal or bird had somehow sneaked in and was the source of these sounds. I therefore got up from the table to find out from where it originated. It appeared that it came from somewhere near the shaft adjacent to the dining room. I also made out that the sound vaguely resembled the musical ringtone of one of these modern gadgets. The rabid rationalist in me simply went on to check the latest mobile phone recently gifted to me by my near ones. But I found that it was lying totally silent in the kitchen. Nor was the microwave giving its musical beeps to tell that the assigned job has been done. In any case, I knew that this was not our microwave beep. Actually this possible culprit had not even been switched on.

My mind started exploring other possibilities. I became more and more aware of the fact that I was the sole occupant of the two and a half-storeyed house. Maybe the strange music came from the portions on the first or second floors. The first floor was occupied by an NRI family who used it as an Indian holiday resort when they make their occasional visit to their home country. It was not their holiday season and there was hence no one staying on the first floor. Further they were very particular to switch off their electricity connection before locking up their portion. The half-built second floor was of course in our possession. It was indeed habitable in the sense that it contained all the furniture and other gadgets necessary for ordinary living these days. But we put that portion to use only when we have a large number of guests staying over for a family ceremony or so. And for the past few months, that eventuality did not arise. Nor could it be that there was some short-circuiting of electricity there causing one of the gadgets to set off the alarm. This was so because I was familiar with those alarm beeps and could vouch for it that the music emanating cannot be attributable to such a beep.

Despite taxing my hard disk to its fullest extent, I could find no reasonable explanation for the music which was showing no signs whatsoever of abating. Slowly, I began to realize that the music was growing even louder. I tried to decipher the reason for this. I made out that the two stray dogs that usually hover on our courtyard had added to the crescendo by joining in. This gave me more creeps because, being a lover of dogs, I knew that dogs have extra-sensory perception. My wife's words that our house has been built on the graveyard of a lady, who was a highly talented one culturally, started ringing in my ears. The irrational thus began getting the better of the rational in me. To prevent that from happening, I looked up to seek the help of the Almighty and my eyes accidentally fell upon the wall-clock. This reminded me that I had to leave home immediately for an important appointment. Ignoring the music all round, I rushed out, locking the house.

I was so bogged down with work the whole day that I did not have even a moment to think about the strange happening at home. I could return to my nest only around 9'o'clock in the evening. To my surprise, I found that the stray dogs, generally there outside when I return, were simply not there. This bothered me a little and on opening the door, I got really upset because the music was still on. I do not believe in ghosts, but somehow the persistent music seemed scary. In any case I did not want to sleep in a place where music was continuously being played.

For a few moments, I was in a real dilemma. A little cool thinking made me realize that fortunately, I was not in a TINA situation. I quickly grabbed my dinner and put it in a plate. I took another look at the dining table to shout at the ghostly being playing the music 'to hell with you'. I darted out of the room and in a jiffy shut the door. There was look of triumph in my eyes, when I locked that ground floor door. I had decided to go the second floor, eat my dinner and sleep in peace away from, and hence undisturbed by, the persistent and ghostly music. I was of course a little bothered by the continued rumbling of this music all the way along the stairs leading to the second floor. But the confirmed optimist in me dismissed these as mere figments of imagination of a person who was dead tired.

On opening the second floor door, I felt as if I had jumped from the frying pan to the fire. There was music all round there and it was even very much louder than that on the ground floor. I had half a mind to beat a hasty retreat, go all the way down, locate a friend or a relative and spend the night at their place. But then on second thoughts, I felt that it would involve too many explanations and too much of bother and inconvenience to all including myself. There was thus simply no escape for me from this ghostly situation. The writing on the walls all around the house was crystal clear. It was in my destiny to confront and if possible nail the ghost. Left with no choice, I picked up courage and embarked on my mission.

I was on the verge of making a mental list of all the electrical gadgets to check prior to grudgingly admitting the possibility of the supernatural. Before I did that, my eyes fell on the new electric bell fixed on the inner door. I was not aware that my people had replaced the old electric bell for the second floor with this new one. I had therefore not heard it ring earlier. Short-circuiting – courtesy the monsoon – had done the rest.

2

The Masked Man

With winter in the offing, there was already a nip in the air in Delhi. What made things worse was the heavy smog that had enveloped the city. There were hence very few people on the roads in the small hours of the morning.

Along the main road of the colony walked a man who looked every bit a ruffian. He was clad in a very old fashioned track suit which ill-fitted him. While his attire was blue in color, he had an odd-looking woolen cap which was brown. The multi-colored canvas shoes that he wore had even a streak of red on them. To crown it all, he wore a white mask which covered his entire face. Since he wore thick and dark-rimmed glasses, even his eyes were not visible.

He was not tall, but was extremely well-built. There was no doubt that if he wanted, he could without difficulty break into most of the glass or even wooden-doored houses and shops located on the road. From the unusually slow gait of his and the careful manner in which he looked at the nameplates outside the buildings, he seemed to have every intention of carrying out such a plan.

He stopped in front of the two banks which were located on his side of the road. One was an Indian one and the other, a multinational.

He looked at the one and then, at the other. It was clear that he was toying with the idea as to which one to enter. After some dilly-dallying he chose, as most Indians would do, the multinational one. Because of his intrinsic skill and earlier experiences of this kind, it was a matter of a few minutes before he could lay his hands on a considerable amount of cash.

He was not prepared for what happened next. Suddenly from nowhere, there appeared an armed guard, who came near him and firmly ordered "Just remove your mask". He was quite unwilling to do so and reveal himself. This slight hesitation on his part made the guard almost point the barrel of the gun towards him and roar "Take that blessed mask off".

The poor guy, caught in the act had no choice but to obey the Lord and Master of the ATM booth. But at the back of his mind was his Doctor's stern advice "Always keep the mask on to escape pollution in the mornings"

3

The Third World War

"If you bloody well can't stand in a queue, *budhe* (A somewhat derogatory term of address when talking to an old man stressing the fact that he is chronologically aged), how on earth are you going to drive?" "I may be thrice your age, but I challenge you that I can drive far better and even much faster than you, *chokre* (A rustic form of addressing of a young lad by older people)".

A burly thirty-year old, standing forty-seventh in a line of eighty odd persons for the renewal of driving licence, was spewing venom. He was furious at a fragile octogenarian standing in the separate line for senior citizens/ladies. The octogenarian was insisting that the general practice of treating this queue at par with the general queue be continued. The thirty-year old was shouting that, in the prevalent context, this was being patently unjust. He pointed out that he had been standing in the queue for two hours while many seniors/ ladies who came very much later got their work done and went away. He loudly regretted not bringing senior/lady members of his family to get his work done much more quickly. In sheer desperation, he came out with a solution. He openly declared that those in the special queue should get their turn only after six persons from the general queue were attended to. This suggestion was loudly cheered by all in the general queue. It hence got the acceptance also by the person sitting at the counter. The faces of those, including that of yours obediently, in the special queue, naturally fell.

It will take me almost another year to join the 'old old' gang à la demographic parlance. It is true that I am past seventy-nine and am less capable of hearing evil these days. But I am able to move my limbs freely and am thus otherwise of sound body and mind. When my driving license became due for renewal, I hence decided to try for it. I went to the office of the Transport Authority and was at the penultimate stage of the usual rigmarole in this regard. Seeing the battle of generations on at the counter concerned, I chose to join the general queue. My problem was that I not only was old, but showed clear tell-tale signs of age too, however. The hair on my head started thinning from the age of thirty-five. As soon as I turned fifty, I started needing spectacles. The few strands of hair still left on my head have been sheer silver for almost two decades. The appearance of wrinkles on my face a couple of years back made the picture even more perfect. People standing in the general queue therefore insisted that I do not join them. They wanted me to go and join the queue for senior citizens/ladies. I was hence, in a sense, constrained to do so and was actually heading this queue when this new decision was taken.

An immaculately dressed and exotically perfumed senior coming originally from Punjab was standing just behind me in that line. Though we were from different regions of India, we had one thing in common. Both of us came from the martial races of India. But for some strange reason, the martial instinct was one that never blossomed in my case. And the little of it that might have cropped up seems to have got mellowed considerably with age. It was true that my smiling face turned grumpy at the announcement. Besides that, all I did in protest was to gently murmur against it. In the case of the gentleman just behind me, things took an entirely different turn, however. He became all sound and fury. He reminded everyone of the Indian tradition of respecting the elders. The vociferous response to this was that the elders in India are known the world over for the special consideration and sacrifices that they make for the younger generation. A youngster even shouted,"Have you become senile, old man? From the way you behave, how can anyone respect you for your age? Have you conveniently forgotten that one must first deserve and only then desire?" The senior was simply touched to the quick at this counter-argument on moral grounds. He fumed, "The government has, through the notice put up here, stated that there should be a separate line for seniors/ladies. I shall hence insist on my legal pound of flesh." The *thuthu main main* (a heated argument between two persons when they are turning abusive) stage was soon reached between him and some from the general line.

It was with considerable difficulty that I prevented an inter-generational fracas. I could somehow make all willy-nilly agree that after attending to three persons from the general queue, one person from the special queue will be catered to. I waited patiently for my turn to come according to this arrangement. But by the time it came, things had literally come to a head. The general queue had almost doubled in length with the people standing in it becoming almost pugnacious in protecting their rights particularly with the lunch hour fast approaching. There was a unanimous demand from them that the old golden rule of 'one after six' be followed again in view of the changed conditions. The person at the counter was on the verge of agreeing. This was enough for the simmering volcano to erupt.

In a jiffy, three different hands with necessary paraphernalia were before the person at the counter. One of these was mine. Another belonged to the person who headed the general line. Not to be left behind in the melee, the martial race representative also forced his hand into the narrow opening of the counter. Fortunately the counter guy chose to attend to me first. The moment my work was done, I somehow managed to wriggle my hand out of the counter and showed a clean pair of heels to be as far away as possible from the intergenerational war on, in full swing.

4

Pineapple Maniac

Rema had enough reasons to believe that her better half – Raman-must have been born as the owner of a pineapple farm in all his previous births. This is not surprising because Raman's attachment to the pineapple was simply profound. Pineapple was his nectar, and his caviar too. If drinks are served and there is pineapple juice available, he would not spare a glance even at the choicest of whisky. At any meal, if there is any dish containing pineapple, he would simply grab it and gobble it up even if it is not properly cooked or well-prepared. When he warms up after a couple of pegs of whiskey, he confesses to his friends that his sweetest dreams are not of sexy women, or of winning a lottery, but about having pineapple as an item in his meal.

Though Raman and Rema made a happy couple, Rema was somewhat different in her approach to 'pineapple', however. It was indeed true that she did not mind an occasional bite of a piece of cut pineapple. But hardly anyone will dispute her view that it is a fruit that is most grotesque in appearance. She would naturally not buy it since she hated the very sight of it. Another strong complaint of hers against the fruit was that it took too long to cut it and get it into a shape fit enough to be consumed. True that both these arguments held water initially, but when fruit and vegetable shops started selling pineapple with its skin chipped off, they totally lost their relevance. Though

Rema then condescended to look at them and even considered purchasing them, she confided in Raman that she hated the idea of getting the little gentle pricks in her mouth while chewing her pineapple piece. In her considered opinion, a fruit which gives you even this gentle tickle while eating can by no means of imagination be termed a sweet fruit at all. To crown it all, she would hammer in the point that it contains none of the essential nutrients in sufficient quantities like the good old apple nor does it have any medicinal qualities like the famous papaya. In any case, it was Rema who had the last word with regard to the fruits and vegetables to be bought and used.

Add to all this the fact that pineapples were not easily available throughout the year in most shops in Delhi. There were however a few months during which they abound in the city. Even in those pineapple days, there was never any question of the household freaking out on the pineapple. Actually, the modus vivendi of the household was such that it was bought at the most once a year. That too was the result of persistent requests from Raman and despite covert and, at times even overt, opposition from Rema.

Rema's eyebrows were hence naturally raised and her forehead wrinkled when Raman walked in with the second pineapple of the year. She sincerely repented the idea of requesting Raman to buy fruits that day. She was not at all happy at the sight of her 'sworn enemy' in the fruit tray. Being a peace-loving person, she was in no mood to raise a furore. But she did succeed in wreaking her vengeance in her own way. She sliced the peeled pineapple into such big pieces that any normal human including poor Raman would find it quite difficult to put any of the pieces into their mouths to comfortably chew. Raman - not too good at cutting things- was constrained to cut the 'cut pineapple' into smaller pieces before sitting down to enjoy his favorite fruit. Since Rema refused to take more than the smallest of pieces cut by Raman and that too for courtesy's sake, the medium sized pineapple lasted for more than three days.

On the fourth day in the morning, Raman opened the fridge to find to his glee a fairly big slice of pineapple still left. He was dreaming of having it along with the usual insipid toast to make his breakfast less unpalatable. But in Raman's case, dreams of this kind seldom came true. After his morning chores including the leisurely and detailed reading of the daily newspaper, he was on the verge of sitting down for breakfast with his mouth 'pineappling'.

A big thud outside the house made him open the door to find out what was happening. To his consternation, he found that the refuse bin kept outside had been toppled. He went out to further examine how this event occurred. He noticed a troop of monkeys walking through the outer balcony. He could easily make out that a member of this army was the miscreant. What happened next literally broke his heart. An alpha male among them was carrying his pineapple piece, munching it with great delight.

Rema had decided that the pineapple had become too old and thrown it into the refuse bin deeming it unfit for human consumption.

5

Damp Squib

Salil's desperate efforts at making some hair appear above his upper lip bore little fruit. There was hardly anything to be seen there. This was despite shaving on successive days. There were one or two strands visible on his chin however. This upset him very much because all other fifteen year old class mates of his had at least half a dozen of these. This lack of hirsuteness was more than compensated by his being six feet two inches already in height, taller than all his classmates. He was actually half an inch ahead in this regard compared to his eighteen-year old, college-going brother Anirudh, known for his muscular frame and fiery temper. Whenever the two boys are left together for more than a minute, there will be loud arguments before Salil shouts for help to prevent being assaulted by Anirudh.

These two teen-agers had to leave home early morning around the same time on all working days – one for school and the other for college. Their mother Anita, by nature highly strung, has become all the more so after a recent bout of serious illness. Her husband Ashish is sugar and honey to all except very near and dear ones, on whom he lets off all his pent-up steam by loud screams. The morning scene in the household is thus one described by the boys' maternal grandparents, staying with them, as one of World war 3. This often constrained the two seniors as well as their pet dog to withdraw from the scene temporarily to prevent the situation from getting even worse.

On one such morning after the usual rigmarole, the boys had left and there was peace all round. A minute or two after that, the door bell rang. This was not something unusual because one of the two boys would forget something or the other, necessitating his hurried return to collect the same. This would of course lead to the resumption of gunfire all round. This storm after the calm is often more intolerable than the original one. Visualising this terrible eventuality, the grandparents deemed it proper not to answer the bell. When it rang again, Anita emerged cursing under her breath and shouting why no one else was answering the doorbell. Since no one responded to her words, she had no choice but to grumpily come and open the door. The grandparents also ventured to peep out of their room in the meantime to find that their worst fear had come true. Standing outside the main door was Salil.

Shuddering at the thought of the disastrous consequences that would necessarily follow, the grandfather beat a hasty retreat with their pet dog in tow. The grandma was concerned and was quite inquisitive to find out what was happening with the intention of helping out if possible. But the grandpa gently reminded her of the possible storm likely to brew outside. This made her decide that discretion was the better part of valor. But both were surprised beyond measure when complete calm prevailed outside for the next ten minutes. At the end of that, there was a gentle knock on their door. Not knowing what to expect, they opened it to find a hassled Anita there. They were really at their wit's end when Anita went on to request the grandpa who was getting ready for his morning walk ritual to take Salil for a walk with him. Since he was a doting grandfather, he could not say no though he did not know what he would be in for.

The grandpa got ready, opened the door, called Salil and the two began their walk. After they had walked a little distance the gradpa gently broached the matter with great trepidation. He wanted to know what made Salil come back and then follow it up by not going to school.

The octogenarian heart attack survivor almost had another stroke, of joy, at the answer "Appuppa (grandfather), after I started out, I got an SMS on my phone that the government has closed all schools to-day because of severe pollution"

6

A COVID 19 Day

Winter was having an icy blast in Melbourne with the minimum temperature recorded that day being the lowest for the past twenty-five years. Radha and Gopal, on a short visit to their son and family, were asleep under the quilt. Something made Radha wake up and glance at the clock. Finding that it was already six thirty in the morning, she whispered into Gopal's ears "Darling, is it not time for you to be up?" The habitual early bird Gopal seemed, to Radha's great surprise, in no mood to oblige. He drowsily grumbled,"Darling, to-day is Monday and so, no morning exercise and shave before my walk."

Gopal was, in fact, a great stickler for regularity. This was actually so much so that he was considered somewhat rigid even by his close friends and relatives. Though superannuated years back, he had strict schedules and times for each activity of his. There were hence fixed times for his meals and even for his tea and coffee breaks. He insisted on sticking to these even while holidaying in foreign countries. His pound of flesh should, strictly speaking, have meant many drops of blood not only for him but for others with and around him too. Fortunately this does not happen and he is not dubbed a total madcap. This is because of the fortunate fact that he would follow his watch only after adjusting it to show the time in the country that he was in.

Radha dropped a brick by saying aloud COVID 19 with electrifying effect.

Gopal simply threw all caution to the winds and jumped out of bed. Post-haste, he got into some warm clothing, brushed his teeth, made his morning tea, and was starting off for his usual ritual- the morning walk. He was on the verge of leaving when Radha looked at him again to literally scream "For God's sake, do not forget the mask, unless you want to be put behind the bars in a foreign country."

Gopal retraced his steps and hunted for the mask. With some difficulty he located one and somehow succeeded in putting it on to his face. With a great sense of satisfaction, he was about to open the door and start his walk, when Radha again interrupted him. "You are no better than our youngest grandchild. How often have I to remind you that that this white mask is to be worn when we visit people?" asked she. With guilt writ large on his face he again turned back.

To remove the wrong mask from his face was of course no big deal for him. But, unlike his wife Radha, he was not particularly known for keeping things at their proper places. It hence took him quite some time and a frantic search to locate the mask considered more appropriate for the occasion, however. All that was mere child's play compared to the Herculean effort that was required on his part to put it on. Under the impression that he had done so successfully, he reached the door and opened it.

At that very moment, his son, Samir, out for a walk, returned. The two were crossing each other at the main door of the house. But instead of entering the house, Samir just stood aghast at the doorstep looking at his dad. It was as if just one look at Gopal had turned Samir into a stone. Sensing something wrong, Gopal asked Samir to tell him the reason for the amused look on the latter's face. Samir was constrained to point out to Gopal that the mask was being worn the wrong way. After some argument about the right way of putting on the mask, Gopal allowed Samir to remove it and put it on his father's face in the proper manner. Before anybody else from the house could emerge from the house to make him wear the mask in an even more proper manner, Gopal barged out, cursing COVID 19 for the loss of a few minutes of his precious 'walk time'.

Returning from his walk, he made his morning coffee and sat down to relax on the sofa watching the morning news on the TV. Good things they say do not last forever. It did not take long for another alarm call from Radha. This was to remind him that it was time for him to leave for breakfast. Puzzled, he glanced at the clock to find that it was just eight in the morning. He hence went on to tell her that there were still fifteen minutes left for this purpose.

The poor soul - Gopal - had forgotten that the living arrangements had been literally turned upside down by this raging bull in a China shop - Mr. COVID 19. In schools in Melbourne, e-learning was on. As a result, during school hours, the usual dining portion of the house they were staying in would get transformed into a classroom for one of their two school-going granddaughters. This improvised class room had to be made available from around eight thirty in the morning till about three in the afternoon on days when the school is on. To facilitate this breakfast had to be fifteen minutes earlier and lunch, almost a working one, for the other members of the family.

The news telecast was at its most interesting stage for Gopal. They were covering events in different parts of the world and the focus was on the latest histrionics of Mr. Donald Trump. But Gopal had little choice other than resign to his fate.

Cursing Mr. COVID 19 from the bottom of his heart, he simply followed Radha to the dining table.

7

Crack of Doom Man

Morning walkers like me are usually health freaks. Some find spiritual solace too in this ritual coupled with or even sans yoga. There is also the bonus point of the sheer experience of observing at close quarters the cross-section of humanity constituting this tribe. Being not on the misanthropic fringe, the bonus aspect has been more important to me than the basics.

The 'apparition' that cropped up before my very eyes the other day in the course of my morning walk was something that really took the cake.

I noticed a strange being I had never seen before approaching me. From a distance, it was difficult for me to make out what it was. For a moment I thought that it was one of those domesticated animals let loose to fend for themselves after their productive years by their kind and animal-loving owners. As it got a little closer, there was a clear indication of it not being a quadruped, however. It was a matter of time before it was near enough for me to make out its contours. The apparition seems to be having a form broadly resembling that of a human.

This being, if it could fit in as a specimen of humanity, has to be classified as an unusually strange one. One would put the age of the being as somewhere between sixty and eighty human years. Since it was not in its natural costume, it was quite difficult to make out whether it was a male or a female. The long strands of hair on the sides of its head were all grey. The top portion of the skull was almost totally hairless. But, since some non-males also have bald heads, nothing definite could be said on the basis of this, about the gender of the being. It was also true that it had hair all over its face. From this, it appeared that the being is usually clean-shaven, but had not shaved for the past few days. But then there are quite a few women with facial hair too these days.

Nor could I get anything more definite about the gender of the being from a study of the structure of its physical frame. The being was definitely on the fatter side- more like a rhino than like a gazelle. Since I was seeing only its front, I could not find out whether its hips were jutting out as in the case of a female or not. But I could clearly make out the bulges on the upper portion of its front. The problem was that fat people of both genders would have more or less similar-sized bulges. Satisfying my curiosity about the gender of the being would have necessitated the embarrassing task of a closer look at the bulges. Fortunately, at that very moment 'the being' bent down to pick up something from the ground. I utilized this golden opportunity to peep a little deeper into the bulging portions even at the cost of being accused as a shameless ogler. My task was made easier by the fact that the being was wearing a half-sleeved vest which was almost like a low-cut blouse revealing most of the cleavage. The successful accomplishment of the task did not also provide a clear solution to my problem. I was at my wit's end and started racking my hard disk even harder.

In a few minutes, an idea flashed across my mind. Something that I came across during my second and closer examination of the bulges and the cleavage was bothering me. It was white and fluffy with streaks of black and was right inside the cleavage between the bulges. Since I was only stealing a sly glance, the question of my spending more time to examine this curious object did not simply arise then. But now, with more time on my hands, I explored the various possibilities. In another few minutes, I succeeded in establishing 'the missing link' between the gender of the being and the fluffy object between its frontal bulges.

It dawned upon me that the black and white fluffy objects between the bulges were strands of hair. I am no expert on the science of hair but my general knowledge tells me that the female of the human species would seldom have hair growing between their breasts. It is true that breast implants for women and hair implants on bald male heads are in vogue for various reasons these days. But even in my wildest imaginations can I visualize women implanting hair between their breasts even in a future age with artificial intelligence in full bloom. So, I came round to the view that the issue about the gender of the being brooked no further thought. In all probability, the being is thus a man.

And he seems to have moved in recently to stay in an area located near my residence. For the past fortnight or so, I have been running into him almost regularly during my morning ritual. Because he is somewhat fat and aged, his chest is sagging and can easily pass off as breasts from a distance. These were only the tips of the iceberg of strangeness of this man.

He is the best living proof of Darwin's theory of evolution being totally valid. Even a casual glance at him will convince anyone that we are all indeed descendents of the apes. A normal monkey-ish trait is to be always munching something or the other. Further, a monkey is forever scratching its body. These two binges of his ancestor seem to have definitely been passed on to this faithful descendent. Though he did not seem to be either ambi-dexterous or a south paw, usually both his hands are full. On the left one he holds a small packet of biscuits or *churmure* (Hindi word for salty munchies). With his right he pulls out a piece of biscuit or some *churmure* to be put into his mouth, which is always in constant use- munching. There are interregnums when the packet has been emptied and thrown off irrespective of whether there was a refuse bin at the particular spot where this actually happened or not. But these were very few and far in between. Somehow he always had adequate stock of these eats in the pockets of his highly soiled and terribly old-fashioned trousers.

The manner in which he successfully prevented his pre-historic pant from falling off is also worth mentioning. A rope covered with grime served the purpose of a belt. The loops on the trouser were all fortunately intact. The rope was through all the loops but the problem appeared in tying the rope tightly to prevent the pant from falling off. This eventuality seemed to arise every couple of minutes making it necessary for him to pull the pant up and tie the rope again as tightly as he could. Both his hands were therefore forever frantically at something or the other. In the remote eventuality of one of his hands being free even for a fleeting moment from these chores, it will simply rush to a randomly chosen part of his body on a scratching spree.

His eyes were large and expressive. Maybe they were once glowing and glittery. But now they are always drooping and downcast. They seem to indicate that there is nothing right with the world. There is premonition in them that heavens are on the verge of falling the very next moment. Being a rabid optimist who looks forward to each day with interest and hope, it is terrible for me to run into such a person right in the morning. But the positives in terms of considerable greenery, vast expanse of land, and almost total absence of vehicular traffic made me stick to the route of my morning ritual, despite this prophet of gloom.

It took a few days for my gregarious nature to get the better of my instinctive dislike for Mr. Pessimism personified. Bracing myself for the worst, I approached him with as smiling an expression as I could manage, to wish him good morning. He did not obviously like my disturbing his meal and his face showed some annoyance at my intrusion. He looked up and stopped munching. I was prepared for a volley of choicest expletives to pour forth from his mouth.

Instead, he responded to my greeting with the most divine smile that I had ever seen in my life.

8

Lost and Found

Ramu was a brilliant guy. His educational career was simply superb. His parents were pleased as punch when he got a high-salaried job in the private sector through campus placement in the IIT which he could join by sheer dint of merit. They were shocked beyond measure when, after a couple of years, he simply chucked it, however. He had decided to pursue higher studies in engineering. After completing these, he chose to join the academic profession. While his younger brother with an MBA was known for his immaculate safari suits, Ramu's sartorial caviar was a *khadi kurta* (a loose collarless shirt of a type worn by people in India made from an Indian homespun cotton cloth). Further, whereas the younger brother hopped around driving a BMW, he could not boast even of owning a bicycle. In fact, he could never learn to drive any vehicle. To crown it all, despite having been to all parts of the globe for academic reasons, his road sense was nothing to write home about. He was in fact not particularly fond of travelling. But conditions were such that he was seldom found home. Actually every second day he would be out of town on official work or to pursue family matters.

This poor soul Ramu was on a family mission in Delhi recently. He had begun his journey from a southern state in which he was born and where his parents still lived. He was on his way to a state in the extreme north where he worked. Transport facilities were such that he was left with a few hours time to spend in Delhi. He had a few relatives, including Krishnan, in Delhi and was on very good terms with them. He had hence planned in such a way that he could spend most of this time with them. He was quite Metro-savvy and took the Metro to reach the colony where the relatives stayed. They had shifted their residence to a new place within the same colony Greater Moti Vihar-1. He had their new address too. So as soon as he reached Moti Vihar Colony -the Metro station nearest to their new residence - he got down from the Metro and gave them a call. He got detailed directions to come from the Metro station to this new residence which was only at walking distance from the Metro station. He only had a small wheeler and a backpack with him. He hence chose to walk this distance. Following instructions carefully, he reached the market and also the roundabout near it. From there, he took a turn which he thought was the right one. He should have reached Krishnan's house in another couple of minutes. He walked and walked, but there was no trace of Krishnan's house anywhere. He soon realized that as was his usual wont, he had got lost. He was hence constrained to ring up Krishnan to explain his predicament. Krishnan naturally wanted him to tell the exact location from where he was speaking.

Ramu looked around to find that he was standing in front of house no E 1. He communicated the same to Krishnan, who was putting up at E 146A in Greater Moti Vihar-1. But Krishnan's place was actually not far from E 1. This was attributable to the chaotic numbering of houses in the colony known more popularly as Greater chaos due to this. Instead of creating more confusion by giving Ramu directions to cover the short distance, Krishnan told Ramu to stay put at that spot and promised to reach there in a couple of minutes. Actually he darted out in such rapid pace that he covered the distance in a minute to find that E 1 was a three-side open double-storeyed house.

But to Krishnan's utter dismay, he found that there was no trace whatsoever of Ramu on any of the three sides of the house or anywhere near.

Completely dazzled by the way things were developing, Krishnan was in a real quandary. He knew his nephew well. He was hence certain that there could be no mistake about the number of the house before which he was standing. Nor did Ramu have any tantric or Gogia Pasha-like inclinations to perform vanishing tricks. The fact however remained that he had simply vanished from the location where he was supposed to be waiting to be picked up. Krishnan even started doubting whether the mobile phone had been playing tricks in this regard. On second thoughts, he found that he had little reason to do so because it was almost a brand new instrument. He racked his brain to find out an explanation for this strange happening. He went to the *dhobi* (washerman) standing at the street corner to ask him whether he had seen anyone looking like Ramu loitering around with luggage in hand. Krishnan drew blank there also because the man replied in the negative to this query too.

Krishnan then explored the idea as to whether there were two houses with identical numbers existing in the same colony. He knew that this was not unusual for their colony. What gets done then is that alphabets are added at the end of the number to distinguish between different buildings with the same number in the colony. The knowledgeable *dhobi* categorically assured Krishnan that there was only one house with number E 1 in the colony Greater Moti Vihar-1. The two then put their heads together to solve this million-dollar jig-saw puzzle. They took into specific account that while Ramu was an outstandingly brilliant guy, his road sense was near-zero if not negative. After considerable racking of brains, an idea suddenly dawned upon them. The flash actually came to Krishnan that there might be an E block in Moti Vihar colony which was located between the Metro station there and Krishnan's residence in

Greater Moti Vihar1. On verifying from the *dhobi*, Krishnan found that there existed an E block in Moti Vihar colony too. Putting two and two together, he thought that he had got four and set off again to locate his waiting nephew. This time he was headed towards the house with that number in Moti Vihar colony.

Krishnan was a resident of Greater Moti Vihar 1. He was hence not very familiar with the adjacent Moti Vihar Colony. It therefore took him around ten minutes to locate their agreed meeting spot in Moti Vihar Colony.

The look of relief and acute embarrassment on the profusely sweating face of Ramu on seeing Krishnan had to be seen to be believed.

9

The Visible Hand

In the upper middle class and gated colony where I happen to reside, there is quite a motley crowd. The proudest in their gait and demeanor would usually be the owner-residents and tenants. Who among them would hold the nose higher is a matter of chance and of personal predilections. Then there are whole-time domestic helps in attendance at all hours of the day to make the lives of the first group of residents more comfortable. Though they are also supposed to reside in these very houses, there is often no effort made to cater even to their basic minimum needs. If they are tolerated inside, it will be in some corner - a veranda, a portico or even a loft. At times there are servant's quarters, often make-shift and unauthorized. Even if these are pucca, the room space will be much less and basic amenities, almost non-existent. The usual argument given in defense of this neglect of basic amenities is that they are used to even much worse conditions and compared to those, this is Heaven. There are also part-time domestic helps, who come to work for limited periods and go back to their respective residences- the cooks, the ayahs, the drivers, the private security guards, the gardeners, etc. None of the groups above recognize or even take notice of what they would consider as the scum of earth- the large army of migrant construction workers including small children, brought in possibly by contractors to build houses, since in the colony many of the older single and double-storeyed houses are being demolished and replaced by builder-built multi-storeyed flats. Families of such workers including even infants in arms come in when the process begins. How they rough it out in the premises from then on for a few months in Delhi known for its extremes of weather is indeed a nine day wonder. But that is a matter of supreme indifference to the rest of the residents.

Another set of visible hands that keeps the colony going is that of the sweepers, with whom all other residents- leave aside the migrant labourers - keep a lot of distance and seldom interact. There have always been of course people employed to sweep the streets. Till a few decades back, every household in the colony also employed its own *jamadar or jamadarni* (a man or a woman, from the lower castes and untouchables in Hindu society, who carries garbage from homes to the refuse dump) to collect the garbage from the house and take it to the garbage dump or *dhalao*. It was not that those days the *dhalaos* then were located very far away from the houses. In fact, no household was more than at the most a hundred metres from its nearest *dhalao* even in those days. But street sweeping as well as this job are supposed to be done by people belonging to particular lower castes. Possibly none of the owner or tenant residents belonged to those castes. Because of these strong caste prejudices, it would have been a sacrilege for such a person to be seen carrying the refuse from the house to the dhalao those days. I am no believer in the caste system and my wife is a highly educated academic. But if our *jamadarni* was absent one day and I had to take refuse to the *dhalao*, my wife would insist that I did so late in the evenings and used lonely service lanes for the purpose to doubly ensure that nobody noticed my carrying the refuse to the *dhalao*. The collection of garbage is done in a different way these days in most colonies including ours. A person belonging again to the lower caste comes on a cycle-rickshaw at an appointed time to the doorstep of each household for this purpose. People who move into the area for the first time and are not aware of this arrangement, make their domestic helps carry the refuse from the house to the *dhalao*. Though we have discontinued the services of our sweeper quite some time back, we have not tagged on to the new system of refuse collection for a number of reasons. Since both I and my wife were working earlier, it was difficult for us to be at home at the time when the person came for refuse collection. This coupled with my earnest desire to help uproot the caste system made me successfully insist that I carry the refuse to the *dhalao* daily without making use of the caste-based intermediary, ignoring the discomfiture caused by this to my wife and also the surprised looks by all and sundry in the colony. I am thus known in the colony for my crankiness to carry, on my own, the refuse to the *dhalao* and to give even a friendly smile to the sweepers who look after the dhalao, despite being an owner-resident here for years.

It was true that some of the problems that cropped up as a result of this practice of mine were rather odd. A very skinny and dusky street *jamadarni* – Pushpa-did not particularly like the huge bulk, dark skin and the region of our newly appointed full-time ayah-Vasantha- employed for our grand-children. Pushpa was by nature very quarrelsome and was simply dying to pick up a row with Vasantha. An opportunity for this cropped up when some refuse was found dumped near our back door in the service lane. Pushpa could not accuse me of this littering because she used to regularly see me perform my daily chore. She conveniently put two and two together and inferred that Vasantha must be the culprit. With her broom in hand and in full battle cry, she came to our front door, asked for Vasantha and when she appeared, started shouting at her in Hindi. But then Vasantha knew no Hindi and Pushpa had no inkling whatsoever of Tamil. Somehow through gestures, Pushpa succeeded in getting the basic message across to Vasantha. Pushpa went on to threaten to get Vasantha arrested and fined for this act of hers. Despite her huge bulk, Vasantha was basically a mild being. But, as they say, even a mouse turns back and bites, if hopelessly cornered. The incessant volley of shouts from Pushpa and her dire threats made Vasanta start vehemently denying the accusation. This rather rare spectacle had already started drawing a crowd of onlookers, including a few others who worked as sweepers. I was hard at work inside my house when this ruckus outside diverted my attention. Unable to concentrate, I ventured out and mediated between the warring parties. The task was not difficult because all I had to do was to act as an interpreter. I told Pushpa in Hindi what Vasantha had conveyed to me in Tamil that taking refuse to the bin was not part of a job assigned to her and therefore she could not be held responsible for the littering in front of our back door. Though because of her instinctive dislike for Vasantha, Pushpa persisted with her accusations for some more time, the firm stand that I took in this regard made her budge in the end. She grudgingly left the scene grumbling that the residents should also take the responsibility of ensuring that even their backlanes were kept free of refuse. One by one, the onlookers also vanished from the scene

DIGGING DEEP

10

The Naked God

Homo sapiens differ considerably in their attitude towards God. There are of course agnostics denying things Divine. Many of them are of the view that the world simply evolved with poor God having nothing to do with its creation. Believers in God are also of many hues. It goes without saying that there are differences in this regard between people belonging to different religions. But even among followers of the same religion there are marked variations on this count.

Though I am a Hindu by birth, I do not have an *Ishtadevata* (Word in Indian languages for favorite Deity for a Hindu) As a result, I belong neither to the *Vaishnavites* (The Hindu group that worships mostly Vishnu, one of the three Gods of the Indian trinity of Gods) nor the *Shaivites* (The Hindu sect that worships God Shiva). I also find it hard to choose between the different avatars of *Vishnu-Rama and Krishna (names of Hindu deities)* in particular. I remember causing consternation during *Janmasthami* celebration in honor of Krishna. People all round were chanting *Govinda .... Govinda* (another name for God Krishna) and absent-mindedly the words *Jai Shri Ram* (Victory to God Rama) somehow emerged from my mouth. The tables were turned more recently when at the *Ram navami* (God Rama's birthday) celebration, I had the audacity to say

Krishna ..Krishna. There was also a near battle of sexes when at a *Mata ki Chowki* (a meeting where prayers are offered to Goddess Durga) in the neighborhood, I was somehow reminded of Lord Shiva and blurted out *Om Namashivayah*. (A Hindu prayer chant specifically for God Shiva)

I fall mid-way between a ritualistic idol-worshipper and an agnostic iconoclast. In my childhood days, I used to visit temples because my mother and other elders told me to do so. As an adult I continued the practice because I emerged as a believer in God and was convinced of His presence all round. Logically, I argued that if he is everywhere, He must be in the stone idols in the temples too. Hence, my continuance to visit the temples even as a grown up.

There is one particular temple in the neighborhood that I visit with religious regularity. It is the *Durga Baadi* (a term used in Bengal and most of India for a Durga temple) located at around two kilometres from my residence. When *Durga Puja* (a Hindu festival to celebrate Goddess Durga's victory over evil) is on, one cannot visualize any place in the world noisier than this seat of the Goddess. But at other times, particularly in early mornings when I visit the place as part of my morning walk, the eloquence of the silence prevalent has to be heard to be believed. The environmentally friendly surroundings add further to the spiritual ambience prevalent there. There is a fairly big piece of land between the temple and its compound wall with many a tall tree growing in the compound. There is also a beautifully maintained garden- abounding in flowers and vegetables. The overwhelming majority of the six odd *pujaris (Hindu priests)* employed by the temple are fortunately those who do not act in such a way such as to sully the atmosphere by their loud and loose banter. As a result of all this, I feel the presence of God when I visit this *Durga Baadi* in the mornings.

I find the deities beautifully clothed too. I am not a connoisseur of fashion, but could make out even with my very limited knowledge that the clothes donned were expensive ones. There were gilts galore on them and I wondered whether artificial fibres were taboo since they were not fire proof. My respect for Gods and to some extent pujaris did not allow me to let this curiosity get the better of me so far in life. But since I am the descendent of the apes, another thing bothered me too. There were no female pujaris and I could not help giggling at the thought of a male pujari changing the Goddess' clothes. Dismissing such thoughts as pure and unadulterated sins, I continued my regular visits to the *Durga Baadi* for my prayers till I got a shock of my life the other day.

I could just not believe my eyes when I found that the glittering clothes that used to adorn the Gods and Goddesses were simply not on them that particular day. Sacrilege thought I. How could Gods and Goddesses be allowed to stand in a temple without their finery? If streaking is a criminal offence in any part of the world for humans, how could it be passé for the divine beings? Or is it that Gods and Goddesses like Presidents of countries are above the law?

These and a thousand other similar thoughts swept through my brain. I had half a mind to see the God and the Goddess without their clothes. But I knew that any attempt of that kind on my part would have meant my committing the worst form of sin deserving very severe punishment not only during my lifetime but also in my succeeding six lives. So, I decided against it.

But God willed otherwise. There was a big thud near the idols. Possibly, something had fallen down near them. This made all the seven pairs of eyes, including mine, turn towards them and commit...... to say the least.....sacrilege.

I was surprised to find that the idols of God and the Goddess actually did not need clothes. The craftsmen, who carved the idols in black stone, had done so in such a way that they had their clothes also carved on to them. The colorful and gaudy clothes that the Gods and Goddesses had on were mere embellishments and were not adorning the idols to cover their nakedness.

11

Who am I?

Identity crisis, thy name is Raghav. The reasons are not far to seek. Born in a far corner of India, he was brought up mostly in Delhi where he settled down and is spending part of his old age these days. There is hardly any stage of his life that he was not confronted with this issue of identity for no fault of his.

It was some decades back that the stork brought Raghav to Trivandrum, the capital of the then princely state of Travancore. On various formal occasions, he has to declare the place of birth. When he mentions it, the people who ask for the information often stare blankly at him. They look hither and thither because many of the present generation have never heard the name of that city. The few brave and helpful ones, who follow up by asking him to name the state to which that city belonged, land themselves in even greater trouble. They simply break their heads looking in vain to locate the state of Travancore in any recent map of India. The inference these "'native place seekers'" draw is that Raghav is either off the rocker or that he is a crook, neither of which is true about the poor soul.

The 'smart Alec'will be quick to point out that there is nothing in a name. No one would deny the blunt fact these are issues often created by clap-trap politicians trying to fool people by mere name-changes instead of meaningful development. To strengthen this sort of argument it will be pointed out that these are not problems serious enough to be considered as part of establishing one's identity, but then Raghav would very strongly differ. This is because he has had bitter experiences in this regard with formal authorities the world over including even postal ones in India. The worst one of this kind that Raghav had was while trying to send important mail by post to that city even very recently because of the name having got Malayalmised into Thiruvananthapuram.

Raghav's efforts to overcome this identity hair-splitting by referring to himself as a *Malayali* (A person who speaks Malayalam, the language of Kerala) lead to even more difficulties. The Travancore Malayalam is different from the Malayalam spoken in Cochin now known as Kochy. True that people from each of these two parts of what is now the state of Kerala can manage to follow the language used by those from the other part. Raghav faces an issue of identity even here because his wife Radha is from Kochy. His Malayalam is hence an amalgam of the language of the two regions, leading to little problems when the couple goes on visits to either region. But when the couple went to see a friend in the northern part of Kerala in Malappuram, confusion got even worse confounded. This was so because the colloquial Malayalam there is often not even understood by most south Travancoreans or even by people from south Kochy.

To make matters worse, if Raghav tries to talk about Kerala at gatherings in that state, he is initially pooh-poohed by others. This is so because he generally is more fluent in English in which language he prefers to start his speeches. But when with some hesitation and difficulty, he switches on to chaste Malayalam as a result and often succeeds in outarguing his opponents, they clutch at a straw pointing out that he has no right to speak on Kerala. They go on to rub in the fact that since he has spent most of his time in Delhi, he has no feel of the nuts and bolts of issues in the *Malayalanaadu*. (Term in Malayalam for the land of malayalis – Kerala)

Claiming to be a *Delhiwalah* (Word in Hindi for a man from Delhi) did not solve Raghav's problem either. When asked by many in the capital as to where he is from, he used to proudly declare that he is a *Delhiwalah*. But then his physique, features and complexion clearly indicate that he must be having links with the southern part of India. Hence this leads to many a raised eyebrow to be followed by a further searching question, as to where Raghav was born with the usual rigmarole about his native place. This irritates Raghav so much that he often asks a counter question as to where the questioner was born. This surprises the questioner who is often one who was born in the immediate neighbouring regions of Punjab, Haryana, UP or Bihar. The person would have come to Delhi a few decades back, but considers himself to be a Delhiwallah while denying the same privilege to Raghav. On a particular day, Raghav was simply flabbergasted even further in the park in his neighbourhood. A senior and educated-looking lady was introduced to him. Actually when told that he was born in Kerala she took it for granted that he knew no Hindi and that he was a Christian. Her surprise knew no bounds when Raghav told her in chaste Hindi that he was born a Hindu and planned to die as one.

To identify Raghav as a Hindu would also be far from the truth, however. He did believe in God and was no agnost. He has of course visited a number of places of worship, including famous temples. But that was more as a tourist. He had no Ishtadevata to whom he would pray for special favours. Nor did he have any faith in ritualistic religion. It is true that he is seen going to two particular temples in Delhi every week. But then, this was to keep a promise to his wife to do so in her company. He felt that God loves all including him and his wife. He was of the view that God was everywhere and was always with him. Extending the same logic, he felt that God must also exist in the idols that are there in the temples. He found solace in chanting *Om* (the sound of the most important spiritual symbol in Hinduism) as many times as possible as a source of comfort. At the height of religious animosities and fervour in India, he actually raised a hornet's nest by chanting *Om* when asked to shout victory to a particular Hindu deity. He would always thank God whenever things go well and think of introspecting when things go wrong. He went all the way to *Ochhira* (a place in Kerala) to see the *Parabrahman (The supreme and ultimate reality underlying all phenomena in the Hindu scriptures)* temple to return disappointed at the sight of people praying to usual idols placed all round therewith hardly any *Om* sign anywhere around.

Proud to be an Indian, Raghav holds his head high in any part of the world. He is very comfortable in foreign countries where the non-resident Indians there flock together forgetting their regional, linguistic and religious animosities. But he finds their exclusiveness due to inability and unwillingness to mix with the local populations, probably not for their own reasons, somewhat unacceptable. This is all the more so because he is also a staunch follower of the *Vasudhaivakudumbakam* (Sanskrit word meaning that the whole world constitutes one family) concept. Within his own country, he goes out of his way to be friendly and hospitable to anyone who looks like a foreigner and seems to want assistance.

It is often said that a tiger cannot change its stripes. But Raghav seems to have done even that in terms of occupation. In the official part of his career spanning over four decades, he was identified as someone specializing in the "Gospel of Mammon". But even there though he was mostly teaching the broad discipline, his interests varied from branch to branch. He was initially interested in applying quantitative techniques into the field, but over time he went on to the sociological aspects underlying most of the issues with his canvas spreading from child health and going on even to problems of ageing.

His friends from his college days still accepted him as one belonging to the broad Economics fraternity. But what he did after his formal retirement made even these die-hards throw up their hands. He went on to creative writing in English and even got some formal recognition in the field. It is true that the horoscopes of people in the disciplines of English and Economics do not generally match much. His former colleagues in Economics look upon him as a crazy outcaste, while those from English Literature look upon him as an unwelcome intruder. In fact he had to spend a few sleepless nights and lost most of his hair when he arranged a function to release a volume of his creative writing at the institution where he had taught, making colleagues from the two disciplines share the dais.

Regarding ideology, Raghav is proud to state the simple fact that though he is left footed, he is no southpaw.

Though embarrassed at times on all these counts, Raghav is not unhappy at the fact that he has no formal identity per se other than being a part of the human race. But Radha feels that if had firmly identified himself with one or the other sociological, ideological or regional groups, he would have soared much higher materially.

12

I have Sinned

For all intents and purposes, I am a happily married man with two children who are now grown up enough to be staying away from us.

My marriage to Usha was a totally arranged one. The bride and the groom belonged to the same Nair community. Common friends and well-wishers of the two families had initiated the process. Each family appointed its own expert to examine the two horoscopes together for the marital compatibility between the two. There was unanimity of view between the astrologers that if the two tie the knot, the couple would have nine out of the ten compatibilities or *poruthas* (Word in Malayalam to depict each of the ten different constituents of matrimonial compatibility, according to Indian astrology) required for marital bliss. Since the bare minimum for a marriage to be astrologically passé would be five out of these ten, the alliance got the green signal. The next step was of course to formalize it by holding a formal engagement ceremony or *Jathakamkoda* (Malyalam term for the formal engagement ceremony at which the horoscopes or *jathakams* of the bride and the groom are exchanged between the elders). Normally in a ceremony of this kind, all that is done is the formal exchange of two horoscopes between the two sets of elders at the girl's house. Neither the boy nor the girl would have any role to play and need not even be physically present. There would be no religious rituals of any kind whatsoever. I was therefore somewhat taken aback at the elaborate manner in which this function was arranged. In my heart of hearts, I was a little pleased because it gave me a chance to interact with Usha a little more. But then the event dragged on and on to become quite boring. A religious priest was present throughout. He made us perform many a ritual un-thought of and unheard of in such a ceremony. Sensing the irritation in my eyes, Usha gently whispered into my ears that all this had to be gone through because her people were highly religious. I was in for an even worse fate at our wedding or *pudavakoda* (*where* new clothes or *'pudavas'* are given to the bride by the groom, during the marriage ceremony amongst the 'Nair' community). This social ceremony with a lit *nilavilakku* (Malayalam term for a big brass lamp lit on auspicious occasions) and *nirapara* (a big round pot, full to the brim with paddy, meant to be a sign of prosperity), usually at the bride's residence, would be totally bereft of religious rituals and intermediaries. The whole event would not have taken more than two or at the most three minutes. For some strange reason, my wife's people decided to hold the wedding at the Laxminarayan temple at Birla Mandir in New Delhi. We first had the Nair *pudavakoda* performed there. But then immediately thereafter, we were also made to repeat the elaborate hour and a half long marriage vows by the pandit. It was only after this long-drawn process that the concluding ceremony- the handing over of the bride by her father to the groom took place.

It took me a couple of years to realize that all this was a deliberate effort on the part of some well-meaning relatives of Usha. They had carefully investigated my father's past. He was known for his intelligence and fiery nature. Though no Casanova, he was notorious for being quite impulsive and fickle-minded in his marital relations. He married a number of times and had three wives already. His first marriage was an arranged one with someone who was a real beauty. But she was not educated and was no match for him intellectually. The marriage, though devoid of happiness, did result in three children.

My father started looking for intellectual solace elsewhere. He came across my mother- a highly educated working woman slightly elder to him. It was a matter of time before they felt drawn towards each other. This made him get a divorce from his first wife and marry my mother. His second marriage lasted for three years and resulted in two children. On some minor matter of little significance, my parents had a petty quarrel. My mother's people, never particularly fond of my impulsive father, made it a big issue. My mother returned to her people hoping that my father will come, make up and call her back. Because of his impulsive nature, my father chose to approach instead his first wife. She said nothing doing till you divorce your second wife and marry me again. Since he was at that particular moment simply furious with my mother, he duly obliged. My mother heard someone knock at her door. Assuming that it was father who had come to call her back from her parental home, she opened the door to find the postman with the divorce notice. His second innings with his first wife lingered on for around a decade and a half and led to two more children. Towards the end of this period, he developed intimacy with a sub-ordinate of his in his office and married her, though there were no offsprings from this union. He was hence quite famous for his four marriages and three wives.

The extra rituals at the ceremonies were calculated efforts by Usha's elders to see that her marriage remained a long and happy one. At the *jathakamkoda* itself, they saw to it that I married Usha according to the Tamilian custom without our being aware of it. Similarly at our wedding ceremony we got married twice, once according to the Nair custom and another according to the *Arya Samaj* rites. I must take my hats off to them for their infallible logic. They had observed me closely and found that unlike my father, I was a God-fearing person. They took it for granted that if I married Usha thrice over and that too two times in the presence of God, I would not dream of leaving her and running after somebody else.

They had not known that what God wills always happens. What is written cannot be unwritten. Destiny cannot be changed. I have cheated. I have sinned.

My marriage to Usha was on the rebound. I was quite involved earlier with another girl. She too happened to be a *Malayali* Nair. But despite this, for some reason, my people were not in approval. Ignoring this, I just went ahead. To an extent, she too led me up the garden path. The so-called affair was never hidden. Friends and relatives from both sides were fully aware of it. I was even indiscreet enough to announce to all and sundry the month and year we had tentatively agreed to tie the knot. It was at this juncture that she decided to dump me by calling off the whole thing. At this my inflated ego was terribly hurt. I swore revenge and saw to it that my marriage took place in the very same month and year that I had announced to the whole world. The only difference was that the bride was not that other girl, but Usha. To be fair to her I made a clean breast of the whole 'affair' to her before the marriage took place.

What I did not tell her was the weakness I had for the dark skin. I am quite dark-skinned myself. Maybe this weakness was a reaction against the jibes I have been receiving on this count since my childhood days. But then this could work the other way round too. A dark person may deliberately go out of the way to choose a partner of a different color to reduce the probability of begetting only jet-black children. This was possibly the reason for my failure to make friends with girls whom I considered black beauties. My experience in this regard was somewhat dismal. I would zero in on such a beauty and start hovering around her. When things warm up a little, she would, however, start looking through me at someone else fair and handsome standing somewhere nearby. Being a robust optimist, I was certain that I would succeed in locating my dark angel someday. But before that took place, Cupid struck unexpectedly and, the rebound too happened. Neither the girl with whom I had the affair nor Usha can be called dark-skinned by any stretch of imagination. I therefore presume that the yearning for my black fairy was an unfulfilled dream at the back of my sub-conscious mind all along.

Usha is a near –reclusive introvert. She hates the idea of meeting strangers. She often shudders at the very thought of making new friends. I was therefore totally surprised when she told that she has a new friend, Cuckie. Curious, I expressed a genuine desire to meet this friend. The chance came in another couple of days. Cuckie chanced to visit us and my eyes could not help popping up when I got introduced. Standing in front of me was the black fairy of my dreams. With chiseled features and an exquisite figure, she was simply out of the world. Her whole frame was darker than that of anyone I had seen before. It even made me think that her teeth would also be black in color to match the rest of her disposition. I hence had to crack one of my pet jokes to make her smile and show her teeth which were glisteningly white. But I still had a sneaking doubt that what I saw before me was an apparition and not a reality. So, I pinched myself to be doubly sure that I was not dreaming. All this left me with not an iota of doubt that I was not.

I cursed my stars for not giving me a chance to run into someone like Cookie when I was much younger. But something told me that it is never too late. In spite of myself, I felt hopelessly drawn towards her. Deep in my heart, I was wondering whether she will mete out the same treatment that black beauties that I had zeroed in earlier had meted out to me. More important than that was the fact that I was a married man much older than her. I hence wondered whether she will respond positively to my overtures at all. But despite myself, I could simply not resist the temptation of attempting to fulfil this dream of mine since long.

Wonder of wonders, she responded. My joy knew no bounds. I shouted Eureka. At long last, I found the black beauty I was looking for. And she had no prejudice against the color of the skin of her lover. The next three months simply flew. We used to meet at least twice daily. Each of us was more articulate than the other in the expression of our love. Extra care had hence to be taken that Usha did not catch us in the act. In all this bliss, I just did not even get enough time to think about where all this was heading for. Not that I did not at least once think òf it. But what I visualized made me shudder.

Like all good things in my life, this also had to come to an end. And it did. It was not exactly the way that I had visualized, however. While on my morning walk, I saw an accident take place. A rashly driven speeding car hit someone and sped away. I rushed to the scene to find the dead body of Cuckie.

I had visualized a *tantrik (a person who practices black magic)* slitting the neck of Cuckie - the lovely black kitten – to placate a Deity in order to obtain some material gain for a client.

13

Who Guards Whom?

It was the last day of 2005. Winter was at its zenith, but being a die-hard morning walker, I was off for my ritual. There was naturally not a soul on the road. Ours is a gated colony and the private security guards both at the colony gates and in front of supposedly residential houses, most of which were being used as commercial establishments, were faithfully performing their duties- blissfully asleep. Even the few stray dogs that look askance at me when I pass, were conspicuous by their absence, having found some cosy corner or the other to escape the biting cold.

I had turned a corner when I suddenly became aware of voices behind me. I looked back to find a group of four young rag-pickers behind me. The youngest was a boy who could at the most be around eleven. The other three were girls and the oldest of these could not be more than sixteen. Their faces were filled with grime and their hair, unkempt. Their clothes - if what they wore could be so described - were torn and dirty. None of them had adequate warm clothing and all except one – a girl - were bare-footed. But despite the deep chill and the resultant gloom all round, they were all in high spirits, laughing and cracking jokes with each other. I could also notice that they were also hard at work not to lose out on the advantage of being early birds in rag-picking. There was a considerable degree of specialization among them. Of the three girls, one was looking for cardboard pieces, another for plastic bottles and the third for other sundry items. The little boy had a bamboo stick, one and a half times his size at the end of which was a round metallic piece, possibly a magnet. His job seemed to be locating metallic pieces with help of the magnet and put them inside a separate bag he had for this purpose.

Having been a pedagogue for decades, I could easily spot the sparkle of intelligence in their eyes. This was also writ large on the manner in which they went about their work both as individuals and as members of a team on a mission. But there was no question of any of them being able to undergo formal schooling which helps to develop their intellects and personalities and also land lucrative jobs in later life. Possibly they are the children of people staying in the slum located nearby. Or maybe they are the runaway children who live on the pavement under the recently built metro flyover and have formed themselves into a team to eke out their livelihood.

Since I am an emotional fool, my heart started bleeding. But then the philosopher in me cropped up to point out, "Hey guy, can you expect anything else in this *Kaliyuga* (Term in Sanskrit in Hindu mythology for the current epoch when injustice and misery are rampant)?" A sneaking doubt, "Why *Kaliyuga* only for India?", remained, however.

I had become too thick-skinned to let these thoughts disturb me for too long. So, I resumed my brisk walk and soon left the rag-picking foursome far behind. I am habituated to taking two rounds of the colony as part of this ritual. I hence ran into this group on my second round too. This was of course at a spot around fifty metres ahead of the one earlier. The team was hard at work with the little boy almost nearing the open gate of one of the houses to examine with his magnet a metallic looking piece which was spotted by him. As

I overtook them, my admiration for the team went up by leaps and bounds.

A fierce growl cum bark coupled with a loud and frightened scream made me turn back. What I saw was something terribly awesome. A spotted stray mongrel- Spotty- was on the verge of pouncing at the throat of the rag-picking boy. The boy's shouts of fear coupled with his efforts to ward off the attacking dog by waving the stick at it worsened matters making the dog more and more aggressive. Things would have taken a real bad turn with the dog literally making mince meat of the hapless lad. But in the nick of time one of the rag-picking girls had the presence of mind to throw a cardboard piece at the leaping dog making it spare the boy. It proceeded to give vent to its fury on the cardboard piece and bit it into smithereens.

To come to think of it, the little boy was duty-bound in appearing to enter the open gate of a house. But then, so was Spotty, forever a good watch-dog. Being a dog-lover, I had found that he used to be the pet of a family in a far-off colony for over a decade. One day, a thief entered the house unaware of the presence of Spotty. He was caught, thanks to Spotty, but in the process Spotty got hit on his right paw by a stick that the thief had. This resulted in his becoming lame and particularly hostile to persons carrying sticks making him fiercer than before. The family had to move out of Delhi and had no intention of taking the old and lame dog with them. So they just took him to a far-off place - our colony- and abandoned him there. Spotty went from door-to-door looking for morsels of food and drops of affection. He was ultimately adopted by this particular family of animal-lovers. They tolerated him inside their courtyard, but never let him enter their house. But after a year of such existence, they went in for a 'decent' pet – a golden retriever. Spotty went into depression for a couple of days, but then having no choice accepted fate. He in fact went to the other extreme and started looking upon the little pedigreed pup as his 'grandchild'. It used to be quite a sight to watch the old and lame dog crawl along with gasping breath to keep pace with the little pup being taken for a walk by the domestic help. This unequal race would finish after a few paces at the end of which Spotty would lay down exhausted by the wayside waiting for 'his' pup to come back after the walk to safely escort him back home again. Spotty would simply raise hell if any other dog appeared on the scene when these escorted trips were taking place. His hostile reaction to the rag-picking boy carrying a stick was therefore most natural. This was all the more so since at that very moment the little pup was already coming out of their house to embark on his escorted walk.

I wondered who was guarding whom and for what? Finding no clear answers, I shut my eyes, closed my mind and putting a lid on to my heart, resumed my walk.

14

Sati Savitri

A tall, uncouth female figure was walking along the lonely road. Well past her prime, she was wearing in *Maharashtrian* (Maharashtra is a state in Western India) style a tattered cotton saree with a terribly soiled and torn blouse stitched in traditional pattern. A 'kind-hearted and charity-oriented lady', finding these to be of no further use, had given them to this woman quite some time back. They must have originally been dark green in color with red stripes, but there were few traces of either color or the stripes left in them now. Having little choice, the woman had gratefully accepted these gifts. She was of course wearing them, but could barely mange to cover her nakedness while doing so. Her hair was dirty and disheveled and her face, covered with what looked like soot. Her protruding teeth showed clear signs of excess chewing of tobacco. They were also living proofs of flagrant violations of even the simplest rules of dental hygiene. Her right hand was almost fully covered with a dirty bandage through which something – puss or medicine- was oozing out. The same was the condition of most of her left foot. But despite all this, she was just walking along pushing a small and empty cart in front of her. There was a desolate look on her face and her eyes looked swollen.

Gopal was taking his morning walk on the other side of the road in a direction opposite to that of the woman. When he came nearer to her, he seemed to recognize her. But she did not notice him and was still lost in her own world. This sign of recognition by him turned into one of shock on noticing that the cart in front of her was empty. Fearing the worst, he crossed over and went near her with a raised eye-brow, wrinkled forehead and eyes full of questions on the empty cart. She looked up, saw him and burst into tears. Pointing towards the empty cart, she said between her sobs *"Babuji, Wohmujheakelechodkehameshakeliyechalegaye." ("Sir, he has left me behind all alone and has departed from this world")**

Gopal had for almost a decade, been running into this couple both of whom suffered from leprosy. The man who had died used to be seated in the cart. His face was terribly disfigured and his hands and feet were bandaged and were in a much worse condition than that of the woman. It was actually so bad that he could not walk and had to be pushed around by the woman- his wife. Gopal's wife Seema generally accompanies Gopal for his morning walks and both used to go out of their way to give alms to this couple. Seema even used to give every year three or four sarees which she had not totally discarded to the woman. Special financial assistance used to be partly provided by Gopal and Seema to this couple whenever the woman sought it for special treatment for her husband whose condition was very much worse than hers. It was with some hesitation that Gopal acceded to the woman's request once for financial assistance to buy a special ice cream for which her husband craved from the Mother Diary milk booth. What decided Gopal in her favor was a gentle reminder from Seema about an earlier incident involving the ailing couple. The woman had expressed her concern about Seema's welfare to Gopal, when Seema was found missing from Gopal's side for a couple of days during morning walks. This had convinced Gopal that the woman's heart was without doubt of pure gold.

Sati Savithri is the term used in a derogatory sense for women who pretend to be doggedly devoted to their husbands without being actually so. Sati in Indian mythology is the lady who jumped into the fire because her father insulted her husband. Savitri similarly is the one who fought with the God of death to reclaim her husband Satyavaan. Gopal felt that if the double superlative Sati Savitri is to be used in a complementary sense, there was none, more deserving this description, than this woman.

Seema was, for a change, in full agreement.

15

The Covid *Thandava*

(The fierce and angry dance performed by Shiva in Hindu mythology.)

To hell with Covid 19 muttered Gopal under his breath.

This murmur of exasperation came from the bottom of the heart of a *'vasudhaivakutumbakam'* (Sanskrit word meaning that the whole world constitutes one family) homo sapien. It emerged because he was being confined to the four walls of his house, thanks to the Covid protocol.

Adding fuel to this fire was another equally relevant irritant for the poor soul. A new family had moved in around a week back to the first floor flat in front and Gopal was yet to become friendly with them. The moving in took place a couple of days before the imposition of the 'protocol' in Gopal's household.

The very next day, while taking his morning walk, he ran into the young daughter of this family out on the same mission. Gopal, never the one to let the grass grow under his feet grabbed the opportunity. After wishing her the customary good morning, he went on to introduce himself in a neighborly gesture. Though he was effusive, he could not but help notice a certain coldness at her end. He dismissed it as the natural shyness of women in India while dealing with men not known to them. He also had a vague feeling that she might have taken him to be a sugar daddy.

Gopal was hence more than pleased to notice an interesting male of the species in that house. This well-built gentleman aroused Gopal's curiosity on many a count. It was a clear case of opposites attracting. Gopal was very much on the darker side, while this person was definitely fair in comparison with most Indians. Gopal was pint-sized whereas this new neighbor was a literal giant. In sartorial tastes too, the two were poles apart. Though no dandy by any manner of means, Gopal was a little careful even about the dress he wore at home. This new neighbor in striking contrast was the very picture of total non-chalance on this count. He was often seen loitering around on his balcony with just a sleeveless vest and *lungi* (a garment similar to a sarong wrapped around the waist, extending till the ankle) on. But what took the cake was the difference in the attitude of the two towards the cynosure of most people these days- the mobile phone.

Gopal, though retired from active service long back, still had a number of friends with whom he loved to communicate. This often took place through the telephone. He did have the more modern gadget, but his preference still was for the good old landline. This was partly due to problems of a technical nature in using the modern gadget in that particular area. Added to this was the difficulty that he had in hearing properly on the mobile phone. Making matters even worse was the fact that he was an unusually soft-spoken person. He had hence to raise his voice to its highest pitch to make himself audible to the person at the other end of the line on the mobile.

The millennials are jokingly described as people who talk on the mobile even during their sleep. The new neighbor, though somewhat older, would fit this bill even more admirably. He was possibly holding a responsible position in an organization involved in carrying out an important project. It also seemed that this "assignment" had a deadline. And this deadline appeared very near needing 24x7 consultation by quite a few with him on many a vital issue. Gopal conjectured all this because irrespective of the time or the day, this new neighbor was always talking on his mobile. And unlike Gopal, he did not have a soft voice. As a result, this semi-clad gentleman was perennially seen walking up and down his balcony bawling through his pet gadget. Because of the openness of the area and the new tenant's loud voice, all around had little difficulty in making out that these conversations were mostly on official matters some of which cried for strict confidentiality. Though few would have approved of this particular trait of the new tenant, it was apparent to everyone in the neighborhood that he was a workaholic par excellence. No one in their senses would hence have denied that his first love was his work. His lawful wedded wife was indeed with him in the same flat, but none in the neighborhood ever heard them ever utter even a monosyllable to each other. This made Gopal jokingly tell his better half that it is the mobile and not the spouse that will figure even as the second love of the new tenant. Gopal racked his brain a good deal to coin the word '*janm-janmkesathi*ness' *(together forever in every birth)* with the mobile phone to describe this behavior pattern of the new tenant.

After noticing that the new tenant was a rabid workaholic, Gopal's admiration for him grew by leaps and bounds. It was a matter of time before, through various sources, Gopal succeeded in unearthing more details about him. It turned out that he was a famous engineer involved in a very prestigious but controversial project. All this made Gopal decide to try to go even out of his way to make friends with this new neighbor.

The very next day, Gopal looked in vain at the balcony for the gentleman to make his appearance. Not one to give up hope easily, Gopal went on to assume that the object of his admiration might have gone out for a short trip to somewhere nearby. Gopal hence looked towards the balcony the succeeding morning also, to draw blank again. Discreet enquiries about the new tenant revealed that he was sick and was in the hospital to which he had taken his mobile phone to prevent his work from suffering.

It was diagnosed as Corona and despite the best medical attention, in another couple of days, he breathed his last. His body was taken to the crematorium straight from the hospital to avoid infection.

Death indeed is the end of life, but then life has to go on. In another few days, the process of vacating the flat by the relatives of the deceased began. The Gopals had witnessed many a moving in and moving out of tenants from that flat. This event should normally have appeared mere routine to them. But even they had to admit that this- the same party moving in and out with hardly any interval between the two and that too because of a ghastly tragedy- was something unusual. When it came to their notice that the items being vacated included a packed air conditioner which was one of the four the deceased had ordered for worldly comfort, but could not be opened and fitted before his call came, the Gopals were really grief-stricken.

The gentle and refined Gopal, in fact, could not resist a full-throated yell 'To hell with Corona'

16

Plot *hee* Plot

(Plots galore)

Advertising gurus tell us that Indian advertising is among the best in the world. One particular Indian ad had caught everyone's eye even decades back. It came out in a written form on the walls in many parts of India. I used to see it along the sides of most railway lines, particularly in India's Hindi belt. It said "Rishteheerishte". It gave the details of a particular matrimonial bureau located in Delhi. Another one that has most recently impressed me talks of "Plot hee plot". This ad seems most catchy now because with a hundred smart cities in the offing all over the country, plots are bound to be much in demand. Ad or no ad, what would take the cake would be the plots that get woven on the destinies of people in real life. I trace some such happenings that took place in a plot in my neighborhood to rub this point in.

The residential colony in Delhi where I put up was a new one when I first moved in. Most of the plots, including this particular one, were hence vacant ones then. Ours measuring around 200 sq. metres was one of the smallest in the colony. It was actually located in one of the smaller side lanes of the colony. The plot under scanner here was one and a half times the size of our plot. Further it was located in one of the bigger roads parallel to the main road of the colony. Around a decade after we had started living in the colony, the owners of the plot decided to construct their residence on it. Being a gregarious extrovert, I was getting a little despondent at the slow progress of human habitation in our colony. I was hence particularly pleased at this development. The owner, whom I had not met yet, was staying in another part of Delhi. He had sent two of his poorer and trustworthy male relatives to stay in a temporary tent put up at the site and personally supervise the construction activity. Since the level of income or education is not the touchstone for my social interaction with those in my neighborhood, I soon started saying hello to them. Though I did not exactly become very friendly with them, we used to say hello to each other. The house being built was a two and a half storeyed one and so it took around ten months for the building to be completed. It was on the verge of completion when something slightly unusual took place.

My wife is quite a presentable lady. But she is no stunning beauty. Further she dresses and carries herself in a most conventional manner. We both were returning home after visiting a neighbor and family friend of ours. I vividly recall that it was in the last week of October. Winter was slowly setting in. Since it was 7.30 p.m., the sun had already gone down quite some time back. Darkness had not fully set in, however. The street lights had not been switched on as yet. We had to pass through the road in front of the house under construction. As we did so, we thought that we heard a rustling sound from inside. We had seen the workers leave when we passed that way en route to the neighbor's place. We were also aware that the stray dogs that used to occupy the vacant plot as their habitat had all disappeared with the start of the construction activity. The mystery got solved when a familiar voice emanated from inside. *"Badshoh, Kabhi aap donom andar bhi aaya karo. Whisky shisky pee lete hai."* ("Sir, why don't you two come in once in a way? Maybe we can all have a drink.") The street lights came on then and we could easily decipher the two caretaker relatives- both almost fully drunk- extending an invitation to us to join them in their drinking spree. I was of course in no mood to oblige particularly since the next day was a working day. The hard nudge that my wife gave me was a very clear indication that she would neither join in nor approve of my accepting the invitation myself. On reaching home, she put me on my guard against the two. She told me how embarrassed she felt whenever she had to walk alone in front of that house under construction because of the lecherous ogling of the two. We both therefore heaved a sigh of relief when the house got completed and these two made their exit.

The owner chose to stay on the ground floor and let out the first floor. To my great delight, he turned out to be a person who was associated for years with an organization with which I too had long associations. It also emerged that like me, he was very fond of dogs. His white Pomeranian – Buddha- with a brown *bindi* (a decorative mark worn in the middle of the forehead by Indian women) almost in the middle of his forehead was one of the loveliest dogs that I had come across. There was general agreement that the dog's name was a total misnomer. Buddha was most unfriendly towards other dogs and had the habit of chasing them whenever he got a chance. A few months after the owner had moved in with his wife and Buddha, I found a small aluminium shed being put up on the ground floor of the house. Curious, I made enquiries. I was told that the couple's son Darshan – a physician – will also be staying in the same house with his newly-wed wife. Further, he intended to set up medical practice there and the shed was being built to serve as a consulting room for him. The old father also informed me that his son was an ardent dog lover too. I was also told that it was Darshan who had brought Buddha to their previous home as a pup and had lovingly brought him up. My joy knew no bounds on hearing all this news. My wife and I were both in our silver years and the nearest doctor was located around a couple of kilometers away. In another two months, the young son of our new neighbor started medical practice from that house. I commented to my wife that we will not die agonizing deaths due to lack of timely medical attention since we now had a Doctor almost at home and she fully agreed with me.

Two incidents involving Darshan are deeply embedded on my hard disk.

It was around 8'o'clock in the morning and I was on my way to the market to purchase something. I noticed a well-built young man in disheveled clothes coming towards me. When he came nearer, I could make him out as Darshan. It surprised me considerably to find that he was actually bawling away. I found this unusual because in most societies men are not supposed to cry at least in public. To make things even more curious, I saw what looked like a bundle of wool in his hands. Something red – possibly blood- was oozing out of the bundle. When he came face to face with me, I succeeded in having a closer look. I could make out that it was Buddha that he was holding in his hands. Between sobs, he gave a quick description of the events that led to this predicament.

It seemed that Buddha was being taken on a leash by the old father for a walk. The two had just started out from their house when a stray dog passed by. Buddha leapt so hard at it that the leash slipped out of the old man's hands. It was a matter of seconds before both the stray and Buddha vanished from sight with Buddha chasing it. Totally upset and utterly helpless, the father beat a hasty retreat to report the matter to Darshan, who immediately rushed out in search of Buddha. After a while, he succeeded in finding a badly injured Buddha lying on the road round the corner. Passers-by told Darshan that the dog had been knocked down by a speeding car. Buddha had not yet breathed his last, however. Hoping against hope, Darshan picked him up and was carrying him home. By the time Darshan finished giving a brief account of the incident, Buddha gave one last gasp and went limp. Darshan was simply inconsolable.

Darshan's father and I continued as neighbours. We do not exchange notes every day, however. We two could hence be referred to more as nodding acquaintances than as bosom chums. The second incident took place a couple of years later.

It was a Sunday and I had more than enough reason to feel relaxed. It was winter and weather in Delhi was at its best. Though it was cold, the sun was up making it an extremely pleasant day. It was around 11 a.m. and I was on my way home from the market. I had particular reason to feel right on top of the world. Shopping from the neighborhood grocer generally puts me in a catch 22 situation. There are solid reasons for this. My wife would win, hands down, high accolades in any brand loyalty contest. And the neighborhood grocer is one who would persevere for all seven lives to ensure that the latest brand is pushed down the throat of his customer. I was dying to get home to get a pat on my back from my wife. For I had successfully resisted by the skin of my teeth the efforts of the grocer to sell the latest brand in place of my wife's preferred brand of toilet soap. But something else, totally unexpected happened in the meantime.

I saw a strange sight on the lane just before ours. There was a haggard-looking, tall and unusually thin man walking with great difficulty. It appeared that he just could not walk all by himself. He was in fact leaning heavily on Darshan's wife. He looked really weird. He was just skin and bones and had little hair on his head. There were three or four people of different ages walking close behind as if in support of these two. This included Darshan's father. I am not a pokey-nosy wanting to know all that goes on in the neighborhood. But this unusual scene got the better of me. I stopped and asked some people around as to what was going on. I was particularly keen about knowing who the gentleman leaning on Darshan's wife was. I did not seem to know him from Adam. And from the way Darshan's wife behaved, it certainly appeared to be someone closely related to her. Another neighbor standing nearby solved the mystery by chiding me "What sort of neighbor are you? Don't you know that Dr. Darshan developed terminal cancer six months back? He has just come back from another round of Chemotherapy."

A month later I got the news of Darshan's demise. After Darshan's death anniversary, his issueless and young widow was sent back to her parental home by Darshan's parents. Maybe she married again. And life went on.

17

Tottering On

Summer is the time in Delhi for morning walks. It is true that when summer is at its peak, around noon the city becomes a burning inferno. But even on those days, there is usually a slight trace of cool breeze in the mornings because there is still some greenery left in what was once famous as Lutyen's garden city. Morning walkers hence abound in all parts of the capital. They are of all hues not only in terms of age and sex, but in terms even of state of health. Along a road leading to a few religious places in one of the gated colonies of Delhi, it is a common sight to see three such ritualists, one of whom is a member of the fairer sex, totter on, each ploughing his or her own lonely furrows.

It is invariably the lady who makes her appearance here first. With a slightly bent back and a somewhat wrinkled face, she seemed to be someone who never sported a smile in her life. Dressed in traditional *salwar kameez* (two piece dress worn by women in India, mostly in the north) with even a *chunni* (A long piece of cloth which is generally used along with salwar kameez by girls) in place, she is often found jay walking in the colony particularly on roads with dividers. On such roads, she generally treads on near the divider in a direction opposite to which the traffic is flowing. It is a real miracle that she does not get knocked down by some vehicle speeding along. Maybe this is because most of her walks are in the morning time when there is not much traffic on the roads. In any case this particular road leading to the seats of God does not have a divider. Further this jaunt of hers generally starts a little before the mad rush to drop children at school begins in the mornings on working days. Her hands are generally clasped together on her back at a point slightly below her hip. Her hair is dark brown with streaks of grey revealing the secret that it is dyed. She thus fits the description of a haggard and decrepit old lady crying for old age care by her 'loved ones'. Maybe she has no one to care for her. Or maybe she was always or had, due to age-related problems, become, too grumpy for her 'loved ones' to tolerate and stand her any more.

The usual picture seen a few yards behind this lady on this road is indeed a very gruesome one. A closer look reveals a male human form in tattered clothes. Though he does not look very old, he has a bent back and walks with difficulty and that too with the support of a stick. He finds balancing virtually impossible and his eyes are always bulging out. He attributes these difficulties of his to a strange and incurable disease that has afflicted him since his very young days. This has made it impossible for him to follow a regular occupation. He is blessed with a sharp brain and succeeded in graduating in Science through correspondence courses. He is often found sitting in parks in the neighborhood with poor school children flocking around him to solve their difficulties in Science subjects and this he does with great aplomb. He has with him always a couple of big and loosely packed bundles consisting of dirty rags and God alone knows what else. What is downright embarrassing is that he sometimes has a tendency to answer his calls of nature irrespective of the place he is in. He is legally the owner of some property in the colony but his affectionate blood relations have usurped most of it leaving him with just a small room with access neither to a tap nor a toilet. His morning tribulation in full public view is to reach a tube-well located near the seat of God. Despite the heavy odds against him, the guy is doggedly perseverant and does succeed in reaching his goal every morning. One is left wondering as to how long his ordeal will have to continue.

At the tail-end of this march-past there usually emerges a typical octogenarian. He is completely bald and the few strands of hair left on his head are all grey. A couple of heart attacks early in life made him go for brisk morning walks regularly for years. He was hence known to all and sundry in the colony for his morning walk which served the purpose of a treadmill test. But with advance in years, age told and brain decay started setting in. He was hence constrained to lessen his pace and go slow on doctor's advice. During his brisk walk days, he was the object of curiosity and even some ridicule particularly by children and senior citizens. In his new avatar, he has gone so much to the other extreme that his philosophy seems to be that slow may make it even if unsteady. He has been actually advised by doctors not to go for long walks alone, but both he and his near and dear ones have chosen to ignore it. An added reason for this could possibly be that his walks included visits to the temple. This particularly pleased his near and dear ones since in earlier years he was never known to be a temple-going guy. His technically savvy near and dear ones got him a mobile phone to be taken with him on his walks. The technical moron that he was, he found the other day that he could simply not get it going when he needed it most at the time of his fatal heart-attack outside the temple of his liking.

18

The Guardian Angel

There are doctors galore in my family. Maybe because of that I am allergic to the idea of visiting a doctor. This allergy turns into total revulsion, if the person at the other end is a star in the super-speciality firmament rocketing from one five-star hospital to another seven-star one while patients needing even primary healthcare suffer in hordes all over. But beggars they say are not choosers. This so since Lutyen's once garden city has now turned into a concrete jungle leading the world in garbage Everests and vehicular pollution. Survival in this veritable hell is simply impossible sans doctors.

The other day I was in such an unenviable predicament. Delhi was witnessing the unequal struggle between emerging winter and receding summer. This war of seasons has an inevitable impact on the physical and hence mental well-being of all. I too developed what seemed to me to be a sore throat. I naturally did what I always do when such things happen- saline gargle every four hours. The blessed cold not only persisted, but even started becoming worse, however. In a matter of days, it became impossible for me even to swallow food. This made me condescend to consult my usual GP for medical advice. But my better half will have nothing of it. She insisted that I go to an ENT specialist without any more ado.

Out went an immediate phone call from my wife to the centre from which I was eligible to get free medical care. To her disappointment it was found that there will be no ENT specialist available there that day. I was quite relieved, but saw to it that no trace of this happiness showed on my face. But my wife was not one to accept defeat easily. She is generally critical of the exorbitant consultation fees charged by specialist consultants in private hospitals. But throwing that to the winds, she went on to ring up the private hospital in our neighborhood. The purpose was to find out whether the hospital has an ENT specialist. My luck was out because the reply she got was in the affirmative. I still continued to clutch at a possible last straw. I offered secret prayers to the Almighty to ensure that it is not the day of the weekly visit of the ENT specialist to the hospital. But no God in any religion would ever listen to a confirmed sinner like me. The information obtained from the nursing assistant of that hospital was that the person – a stickler for punctuality – is there every day between 9 and 12 in the mornings. To make matters even worse was the fact that it was already 8.30 a.m. My wife was after my blood to ensure that I leave immediately to meet the specialist and be the very first patient that the specialist meets and examines.

Because of my earlier experiences about the lack of punctuality of such specialists, I dilly-dallied my utmost and was outside the specialist's room full fifteen minutes later than the person's scheduled arrival time. But despite this, my worst fears came true. There was no trace whatsoever of the person. This bugged me considerably. Morning is the time I peak. Further I am a stickler for punctuality. I therefore hate the idea of wasting time in the morning waiting for someone coming in late. Having little choice, I had to do what I detest most for five long minutes. At the end of it, fuming from inside, I went to the reception to curtly ask them what time the 'busy' specialist is expected to arrive. After a few unsuccessful attempts, contact was made with the specialist and the information obtained that true worshippers have to wait till 10 'o' clock for the *darshan* (an opportunity to see a holy person or the idol of a deity). Since I was not particularly keen to have this, I had half a mind to call the whole thing off. But that would have meant turning my usually gentle and mild wife into a veritable Durga– a prospect I shudder to think of.

I hence simply headed home, undecided. My better half was eagerly waiting to know the result of my meeting with the specialist. Though a little unhappy at what happened, she simply blew her top when I threw a mild hint that I may not follow up the idea. When the clock neared a quarter to ten, she naturally started reminding me of my need to visit the hospital. I could not successfully avoid being pushed out of the house for this purpose beyond half past ten. Nor did I have better luck this time in meeting the visiting specialist. There was no trace whatsoever of the person. Attempts by the receptionist of the hospital to contact the person on phone to communicate that a patient was waiting also met with little success. In desperation, the receptionist left such a message on the specialist's mobile phone. This did have some impact because back came a message that the specialist would be reaching the hospital any moment.

The volcano of anger inside me at all this was waiting to erupt. This was all the more so as I noticed that I was the only patient in this boat. I began pulling up my sleeves to give a big piece of my mind to this highly irresponsible specialist who seems to have thrown professionalism and oaths of service somewhere by the wayside.

My eyes fell upon a harassed looking young lady with bobbed hair rushing into the hospital. It appeared as if something recent had drained her of all her energy. Misery they say loves company. Since I was also in a more or less similar situation I felt a sneaking sympathy for her. This became all the more so since she appeared heading straight towards the specialist's cabin. At long last, thought I, there is another patient too waiting for that rare breed. But wonder of wonders, instead of waiting outside with infinite patience, she just opened the door and was about to enter the cabin. For a moment it seemed to me that she is one of those nouveau riche snobs. These divine beings would deem it a sacrilege to stand in lines meant for ordinary mortals. What happened next made me feel that there is still some hope for the human race however.

On seeing me waiting outside the cabin, she stopped short. Turning to me she said in a creaking voice "I am terribly sorry to keep you waiting. There is turmoil in the town due to which the schools got shut. I was constrained to rush in bumper-to-bumper traffic to bring my son back home from school." She went on to give the most thorough examination that I ever had from a specialist.

This incident made me learn the pleasant way the dangers of trying to stereotype people.

19

Heart Overcomes Space

Gopal and Radha are typical representatives of the former globalised world. Their only son Ramesh, his wife Menaka and their sole issue then – four-month old Enakshi - left India around a decade and a half back in search of greener pastures. After trying different permutations and combinations in terms of countries and cities within each, they seemed to have finally settled in Sydney in Australia. During this period, they had two more kids. Both of them were born in Auckland, New Zealand. One of these is a daughter Vinita, a year and a half younger to Enakshi. The youngest of the three kids is a lovely boy named Aaditya whom the stork brought around twenty months after Vinita came into this world.

Ramesh insists that his parents spend at least a few months every couple of years with him. The two octogenarians, despite having had a sense of surfeit of foreign travel during their working lives, willy-nilly oblige. This is partly due to their fondness for their grand-children. It is not that they do not have grandchildren in India. Their daughter is settled in India with her family which includes her two teenage sons. But the only granddaughters that they have are the "kangaroo" ones- Enakshi and Vinita. And no one can dispute the fact that a granddaughter is a totally different cup of tea compared to a grandson.

One of the additional reasons of the elderly couple visiting Sydney was to have a feel of the newly acquired house of Ramesh and Menaka. From the e-mails and photos they got, it was clearly a much bigger one than those that this younger couple had occupied earlier. This was a definite convenience, because in those houses the children did not have independent rooms and even sufficient space to carry on their studies comfortably. Since the older couple had spent their working years in the teaching profession, they placed a high value on formal education and hence on this basic pre-requisite for the same. They were therefore quite concerned about this lack of basic amenity for their grandchildren earlier in Sydney.

As a result, when Air India offered highly concessional rates for a trip from Delhi to Sydney and back, the aged couple could just not help grabbing it. They left India on a three-month visitor visa on the 21st of February 2020 in the afternoon to reach Sydney on the 22nd early in the morning, after a fairly comfortable non-stop flight. It was hence with a smile on their lips that the two embraced their grandchildren at their Sydney residence on the 22nd morning. But the arrival of the grandparents in this new house at Sydney necessitated considerable readjustment in the existing living arrangements there. Ramesh and Menaka had even earlier decided that the portion that Enakshi occupied would be given to Gopal and Radha with Enakshi shifting to the room that Vinita was having, with the two sisters sharing it. This was done so that the aged couple could have their independent lives and still be part of the extended family. The portion given to the grandparents and formerly occupied by Enakshi consisted of a bedroom, kitchen, drawing room, bathroom and toilet replete also with all other necessary amenities. The grandparents were not particularly happy at this disruption in their grand-daughters living arrangements, however. But since Ramesh and Menaka were insistent on this, they willy-nilly agreed.

In their heart of hearts, however, they were somewhat perturbed at this. They did know for certain that the two sisters were the best of friends. But then, the two were slowly getting used to their independence and privacy and were both in their touchiest years-early teens. To make matters even worse was the fact that there was only one wardrobe which was inside the bedroom in the portion being given to the grandparents and most of Enakshi's clothes were kept in that. The result was that Enakshi had often to wait for considerable periods outside the bedroom when the grandparents were changing or were in the middle of their morning rituals. At times this happened in the morning hours when she would be in a hectic hurry to get ready for school and reach there on time.

The grandparents were hence genuinely worried as to whether this visit of theirs would in any way lead to better inter-generational bonding. In fact, they were all the more concerned because during their earlier visits they had noticed that Aditya was more Australian in his accent than most Australians, making it very difficult for them to make out what he was saying. Due to all this they were even afraid that this visit may result in the exact opposite with the grandchildren looking upon them as unwanted intruders on their privacy and comforts. They had in fact seen one of their Indian friends, a widower, when he goes abroad to stay with his son and family for short periods annually, face this ordeal. The spoilt grandson in particular was so nasty that he would openly hurl abuses at the 'poor' old man. He did complain to the parents about this atrocious behaviour, but these produced hardly any results. The lame excuse used was that these were just passing teenage blues.

It was of course true that the experiences that Gopal and Radha had with their NRI grandchildren earlier were of a totally different kind. But then the three were all very small kids in awe of, and overflowing with affection for, their grandparents. The million-dollar question in the minds of the old couple was whether the attitude of the grandchildren towards them would have undergone a qualitative change as a result of the teenage blues that some similar NRI children were experiencing. It was hence with considerable trepidation that they ventured out on their current foreign jaunt.

The aged couple had not taken into account the fact that there was something unusual about their grandchildren and with Enakshi in particular. Gopal had noticed this unique spark in her even during a visit of theirs long back. The little girl then had taken up cudgels for her grandfather when her mother had inadvertently been somewhat curt in her dealing with the old man. In fact Enakshi was one of those rare persons who not only had strong values and convictions but also had the courage to pursue them. The grandparents could never forget also the unusual incident involving Enakshi when she was around three. It happened when Menaka and Ramesh had gone out leaving the two sisters alone in the house. Vinita, who was not even a year old then, answered her second call of nature. With no hesitation whatsoever, Enakshi went on to clean up Vinita and change her nappies. Menaka and Ramesh could not contain their tears of joy when Enakshi told them about this on their return.

The fears of Gopal and Radha on this count turned out hence to be totally false and unfounded. Enakshi, despite entering her teens, continued to remain the girl with a heart of gold. Normally girls of her age would have sulked and maybe put on even grumpy faces on being displaced from their usual habitats. But not, Enakshi. The usual divine smile usually on her face continued to remain there even when she had to wait sometimes for long to try her dresses on to decide which one to wear. The original two- month stay of the aged couple got extended to seven months – courtesy Mr. COVID- 19. But even this produced no trace at all of any resentment on Enakshi's face. In response to this development what she did was something unusual. She went out of her way to make special dishes for her grandparents and that too after asking them what they liked best. And one of her natural flairs was in the field of culinary art.

No wonder Gopal and Radha came back to India after their stay with their grandchildren not only with their hearts overflowing with joy, but also with expanded waistlines.

CHURNINGS

20

Touch Me Not

The ground floor flat in which we reside these days is part of a small and compact four-storeyed structure. This building is on stilts, has no basement and each floor consists of only one flat. The complex abounds in cars owned by residents, however. The family occupying the top floor is a nuclear one, but has a flair for cars and owns four of them. Joint families occupy the other three floors with there being two cars per flat for obvious reasons. Besides providing parking space for these ten vehicles, the stilt area also serves the purpose of a lounge for the drivers of these cars. Actually, ours happens to be the only house in the immediate neighborhood with a stilt. As a result, drivers of cars in houses nearby too deem it convenient to join this group of drivers. Further, the part-time maids working in our building and also in houses in the near vicinities, find our stilt area a safe place to sit and relax. This is particularly true around lunch time. In fact, one of the female part-time domestic helps also deems it convenient and even safe to indulge in an after lunch snooze there.

Normally I have to venture out of my flat at least thrice during the day. The lift and the staircase are so located that in doing so, I have to pass through the stilt area. This fact coupled with my friendly nature, has resulted in my having more than a nodding acquaintance with almost all members of this gathering. The composition of this group is of course not the same every day. Till recently, however, there were four- Mona, Bimla, Sonu and Lakshmi Kant –who were all Hindus and were invariably present every day.

Mona is the part-time domestic help who cooks for us and was born in the Samastipur district of Bihar. This fairly smart-looking mother of three in her mid-forties is a dusky extrovert. With a ready smile for everyone, she has the knack of becoming part of most of the groups of persons in similar occupations in the neighborhood. She is very meticulous about observing *Chhat Puja* (A special prayer, standing knee deep in a holy river, to the Sun God, performed in Bihar and surrounding parts, thanking Him for bestowing the bounties of life on earth). She is not a Brahmin and belongs to the *Vaishya* (the caste that used to take care of agriculture and trade) caste. In fact, she is a staunch worshipper of *Shirdhi Sai Baba* (A highly respected Indian Godman who is worshipped by all religious groups in India, is now deceased, and whose biggest "temple" is at Shirdhi in Maharashtra).

Despite her friendly nature, Mona looks upon Bimla - the maid who regularly cleans the common portions of the apartment including the stilt area - as her rival. One apparent reason for this is that Bimla too is adept in cooking and had out-competed Mona for the part-time position as a cook in one or two flats in the neighborhood. Further Bimla is less dusky, a couple of inches taller, a few years younger and has a better-endowed and more proportionate figure. Bimla too is a gregarious extrovert and often goes out of her way to be friendly with all around including the group of drivers. In the process, she takes an inordinately long time to clean the area under the stilts. But, unlike Mona, she does not have the habit of catching a wink in the afternoons in the stilt area. Bimla was born in the Gorakhpur district of Uttar Pradesh and also belongs to the vaisya caste.

Sonu has been a driver with the occupants of the top floor for many years and is more in the nature of a 24x7 handy man. He is from

Bareilly in Uttar Pradesh and is a *kshatriya* (the warrior class). But he is forever proudly proclaiming that he does his *pranayama* (Name of a yogic asana) and other yogic exercises besides *puja* (worship) regularly. Being myself an early bird that goes for a morning walk with religious regularity, I can vouch for his statements. This is so since he has to spend the night in the stilt area whenever the top floor resident has to go out for dinner or for a late night party. On such occasions, when I go for my morning walks, I invariably run into Sonu in action in *shirshasana pose* (a yogic asana) with his head down and feet up in the stilt area.

Lakshmi Kant is the driver employed by the first floor occupants. He is a proud Brahmin from the Darbhanga district of Bihar. Tall, well-built and with a special glow on his face, he takes particular care to see that he is always smartly dressed. My, almost regularly repeated, comment that he should have been with the armed forces pleases him very much. He has mentioned to me that his long tenures of service with many senior people in the bureaucracy and corporate world is the cause of his sartorial fastidiousness. Nor was he in any way behind in the strict observance of Hindu religious rituals. He goes out of his way to point out that, unlike many a Brahmin these days, he never misses his daily bath and the succeeding elaborate pooja for his *Ishtadevata*. At a convenient corner of the stilt, he has even placed a picture of this deity of his and is frequently heard reciting *Hanuman chalisa* (A popular prayer among Hindus for God Hanuman in which forty different names of his are also chanted) while burning incense before it. But whenever he is off duty under the stilt on hot afternoons, he also cannot escape from the seductive charms of *Nidradevi*. (Hindu Goddess of sleep)

Sonu and Lakshmi Kant have between themselves succeeded in procuring a table fan for their use in the stilt. They switch it on almost always in summer and this gives an added reason for drivers in the neighborhood to join in, particularly when they have their afternoon siesta. Mona also tries to catch a little bit of air emanating from that fan by lying down for her afternoon nap near the contraption.

Being a staunch believer in equality, this divine sight in the post-lunch period in the stilt area used to give me great satisfaction and pride. Here is urbanization, thought I, leading to the total annihilation of rigid caste distinctions and also of gender bias in Hindu society. But it was a matter of time before it became clear to me that I was living in a fool's paradise on these counts.

One fine morning, I found something amiss. The usual radiant glow on Lakshmi Kant's face was conspicuous by its absence. I wondered whether he had a fight with his wife that morning. Another possibility that came to my mind was that his morning pooja was disrupted by something untoward. I was on the verge of talking to him with a view to soothing his nerves. He could possibly visualise my intentions. He spared me the embarrassment of finding out the cause for his consternation. Instead he took the initiative and came to me with hesitation writ large on his face. As he neared me, he looked like someone having a hangover. His eyes were groggy and downcast and his face, crest-fallen. But I knew for certain that he was a tea-totaller and that Bacchus could not be the cause for his feeling low. He bent down and whispered into my ear "Sir, can I make a special request to you?" I replied in the affirmative and on getting it, he wanted me to devise some means by which Mona is prevented from spending her free time with the drivers in the stilt area. In his view, the best thing would be for me to bell the cat by letting her know of this taboo.

Somewhat taken aback and disappointed at this gender bias raising its ugly head in this heavenly stilt, I asked him to tell me the reasons for this request of his. He came out with two, both of which were, according to him, quite cogent. The first reason that he gave, did not surprise me one bit. It was that the stilt was a bastion of male drivers and a sole member of the opposite sex – if she chooses to sit with them - is bound to feel like a fish out of water. He pointed out that the malefolk would be unnecessarily constrained in their language, gestures and behavior because of the presence of this 'foreign' element in their midst. While many would consider such a constraint to be a very desirable one, Lakshmi Kant very strongly felt that men should be allowed to be uninhibitedly masculine in behavior, at least for a few hours every day. In his view, this can happen only when there is no woman around. A rabid feminist would condemn such a view as gender bias in this uni-sex world. But I excused him for this argument of his, the genesis of which was that there should be two lounges, one for men another for women.

To drive his point further home, he went on to describe another recent experience of his. This seems to have taken place only the very previous afternoon when they were all having their siestas under the stilt area. It seems that Mona's toe accidentally brushed against the foot of LaxmiKant. Possibly Mona was not even aware of this. But, not so, LaxmiKant. In his view this was sacrilege, pure and simple.

The Brahmin in the man was aroused. He quietly slipped out, went home, had a bath again and carried out further basic *shudhikarana* (rituals for his purification). Fortunately, his services were not required by his employer between 2 and 5 p.m. that day. So he could return in time to resume his official duties again with the certainty that God was still with him. He was naturally inconvenienced considerably as a result of all this and did not want similar incidents to be repeated. According to him, the only solution would be to see that Mona is categorically told to keep herself away from the group. LaxmiKant requested me to bell the cat in this regard. I had to willy-nilly agree to do so for the sake of maintaining peace in the stilt area.

It was with great trepidation that I tried to perform this assigned task the next morning. I had expected Mona to protest at least mildly against this banishment. But surprisingly she did nothing of that kind. On the contrary, she meekly agreed to my suggestion and has her afternoon sojourn elsewhere these days. Maybe she has got so used to the writing on the wall that she did not want to break her head against it.

For the next two days, I could not, however, help noticing a mischievous smile of triumph on Bina's face which almost said 'I am now the Queen of all I survey'.

21

Caste on Exit Mode

Perched smugly on a stool, near our dining table, sat Pushpa, in her early sixties. Countless wrinkles and a haggard appearance made her look at least a decade older. In walked Arup – our fifteen-year old grandson – spending his holidays with us. Though Arup was literally born before Pushpa's eyes, she did not at first make out the straggling and unusually lanky adolescent. This non-recognition was mutual, since Arup and his parents had been mostly out of Delhi.

So, when I warmly welcomed Arup by name, all Heavens broke loose. Pushpa simply could not contain her joy at the sight of the chubby little child of yesteryear transformed into a big-built adolescent. She just gushed forth in sheer affection for 'little' Arup. And Arup did what he had been told to do when meeting elders to show respect for them. He bowed before her, bent down and touched her feet.

This led to pin-drop silence in the room. It almost appeared as if somehow Heavens had fallen. My wife, I and even Pushpa herself had strange looks on our faces. Though nobody said anything, it seemed to Arup that he had done something terribly wrong. He did rack his brain, but could just not fathom the cause of all this pandemonium. With a puzzled look, he slid out of the room.

Pushpa was our *jamadarin* for over two decades. It used to be her job to take the refuse from our house to the bin kept in the colony by the municipal corporation. It is true that ours is an educated family, used to shouting from the rooftops that we are dead against the caste system. In the gated colony in which we stayed, we were actually among the very few who would admit people like Pushpa into the drawing room. Offering her at least a stool to sit there despite her being an old person would have just meant sacrilege to neighbors around. But we used to commit that too.

This was the limit to which the 'broad-mindedness' of the members of our household would go, however. The reason for this is the fact that the sub-conscious minds of all except Arup in the room, had views with very strong roots. Deep within us, there was still a feeling that Brahmins had to be shown respect because of their special training and capacity to act as intermediaries between us and the Almighty. A *jamadarin* would still only be a *jamadarin* - very much lower in the caste hierarchy and hence to be looked down upon. The question of extending due respect for her age by a young member of our household was something just unthinkable even for us. Hence, the stupefied look on everyone's face.

Arup was habituated to going for a long morning walk with me every day. Looking at our sartorial preferences, it was loud and clear to all that we were of different generations. But then we two did have a very good rapport. As a result, during these walks, we have long conversations on everything under the sun. He thus broached the Pushpa episode with me the very next morning in the course of our morning ritual.

I tried my best to evade the issue. But ultimately I was cornered. He wanted to know whether he had done anything seriously wrong while meeting Pushpa. I had to grudgingly mumble that he only did the right thing, though there was a murmur of protest from somewhere deep inside me. Luckily for me, he failed to notice the terrible turmoil in me while answering his query.

Reassured by my reply, he moved forward in life.

22

Warmth in Rags

Cycle rickshaws were never there in the South Delhi colony in which we reside. But with Delhi metro spreading its wings also to this area, things changed. It was soon a common sight to see a big fleet of these parked in front of the nearest metro station to ensure last mile connectivity to metro commuters. People travelling for short distances within the colony also found them to be a convenient mode of transport. It was hence not a rare sight to see a cycle rickshaw or two parked in front of all the three markets or convenient junctions within the residential area of the colony, looking for passengers. On hot afternoons, it was not uncommon to see a *rickshaw-wala* sleeping blissfully inside his vehicle under the shade of trees in some remote corner of the colony.

It surprised me considerably when I found a cycle rickshaw parked in front of one of the houses nearby. This house is located in the middle of a heavily trafficked road, far away from the neighborhood markets. I noticed it because this was the road I frequented for the ritual of my morning walk. The shabbily dressed guy who rides this cycle rickshaw could also be found hovering around the place. This made me wonder whether the cycle rickshaw belonged to the person who rode it. If so, he would have no right to park it at that spot unless he was in some way or the other obliged to the house owner for the purchase of the cycle rickshaw. Maybe the house owner is a good Samaritan who helped a poor acquaintance or a former domestic help become financially independent or make a better living by chipping in part or whole of the finance in this regard. Recent reports of enterprising people in Delhi owning large fleets of cycle rickshaws gave rise to another idea. Maybe the cycle rickshaw belonged to the occupant of the house with the rickshaw-rider being just an employee. Either way, I was a little concerned because only the other day one of the workers in a house under construction in the neighborhood was caught while trying to break in and steal a few things from another house nearby.

Being by nature friendly, I have at least a nodding acquaintance with all and sundry in the neighborhood. It was hence just a matter of time before I was on smiling terms with the rickshaw-walla. A stray dog had given birth nearby and he went on to adopt one of the pups. The extra care that this vagrant took of his newly acquired canine friend was such that he could put many of the so-called 'pet dog keepers' of the colony to shame. He did well in not keeping it tied up. But it was quite a job for him to see that it was not run over by speeding vehicles rushing past. I distinctly remember the frenzied gesticulations that I had to do to make a speeding Innova slow down to avoid running over the sprightly canine. There was another problem too. Pups are very playful and one day when I was passing by, it leapt at me and almost bit me. The rickshaw-wala apologized to me and chided the pup. I then asked him whether the pup has had injection against rabies. I was pleasantly surprised to hear that the poor guy had taken his pet to a charitable veterinary clinic located quite some distance away to get all the necessary injections done. In another couple of days, he started tying the pup with a piece of rope to the low-lying branch of the tree under the shade of which they all flocked together. The rope gave the pup sufficient freedom to move around, but was not long enough to enable it to reach the road or snap at passers-by. Though I appreciated this arrangement, I pointed out to him that this continuous chaining will turn the gentle and friendly dog into a fierce biter. A week passed in this manner. While on my morning ritual on the eighth day, I looked for the pup at its usual spot and found that it was simply not there. When there was no trace of it the next day also, I took it for granted that the rickshaw-puller, finding it too cumbersome to keep the pup, had simply abandoned it as most usual 'pet-lovers' are prone to. When I ran into him a few days later and ventured to ask him as to what happened to his pup, I was in for a pleasant surprise. He informed me that he had sent the pup to his village so that it can roam around the house freely without being tied up.

I continue running into the rickshaw-wala during my morning walks. One day I went for my ritual a little later than usual. I was hence walking at a much brisker pace. It looked as if I had to reach somewhere and was getting late already. The cycle rickshaw-wala was there at his usual spot. He was not yet ready to scout for customers. Before I could give him my customary smile, he made my heart melt by offering me a lift to the place I was 'rushing' for 'work'. After clearing this misconception of his, I gave him a smile that came from the very bottom of my heart and was hence very much warmer than usual.

Epilogue

I was slightly unwell and set out on foot to go to the Hospital in the neighborhood. At that very moment my immediate neighbor emerged in her chauffeur- driven car. She saw me, but did not bother to stop to ask where I was going. The question of offering me a lift, which I would have gladly accepted, would never ever have crossed her mind.

23

The Magpie Sang

There are very few people who deserve the title 'gregariousness personified' than Raghav. He usually resides in New Delhi, once famous as 'Lutyen's garden city'. He in fact loves nothing better than interacting with fellow humans. He is also an ardent lover of nature, however. Even a single flower in his little garden used to fill him with immense joy. Though by no manner of means a great ornithologist, he easily distinguished between the different birds that used to hover around there. In fact, he used to derive immense pleasure in simply watching them.

Despite ritual religion not being Raghav's cup of tea, there was a religious regularity with which he used to perform a particular ritual. Hail, rain or shine, each morning used to see him take a walk alone for around five kilometres. It was of course true that he used to come across a number of other birds of the same feather in the process. It would be quite natural to jump to the conclusion that it was mainly these social interactions with fellow humans that made him embark on these morning jaunts.

But then there are things far beyond sheer logic in life.

The usual rule that a couple in an arranged marriage do not generally develop a good emotional rapport did not apply in the case of Raghav and Radha. He often confided in her sharing also his innermost feelings in the process with her. From these, it emerged that there was a much more important factor goading him on for his morning jaunts. This, according to him, was the feast of avian symphony that soothed his ears in the course of these walks. He found this to be in striking contrast with the repeated honking of cars that would greet him in the concrete jungle in which he now resided. There were still birds galore on the route that he generally took for his regular morning jaunts. He used to particularly look forward to the gentle and amorous cooing of the doves and the simply unparalleled melody produced by magpie robins both of which species abounded along the path that he generally tread for this purpose.

Good things, they say, seldom last forever. Destiny created a somewhat strange situation in their lives. They had gone to a far off country for spending a short holiday with a close relative of theirs. But unfortunately just before their return from there, COVID 19 struck. The resultant flight cancellations, lockdowns etc. made it simply impossible for them to return to their country and resume normal life. Making matters worse was the fact that their relatives had recently shifted their residence to a new locality. They hence did not have even nodding acquaintance with any of their immediate neighbours. They were also not keen, for their own reasons, that Raghav breaks the ice with their neighbours in the unusually cold country down under. The argument put forth by these relatives was that people in that country usually cold shoulder such attempts and never reciprocate. Being mere birds of passage, Raghav hence had no choice other than to let things be. But he saw to it that the modus vivendi worked out included walking a few times around the house taking care that he does not go too far away from the gate of the house.

In this unplanned 'imprisonment' in a far-off land, the greenery around the house in which they were staying provided Raghav with considerable solace. There was no doubt that the family that had built the house decades back and occupied it till the time Raghav's relatives moved in were ardent gardeners. They had actually taken away most of the pots with flowers. But then there were quite a few that somehow got left behind, with the result that there were still a large number of flowers in the garden. The thirteen rose plants in full bloom gave immense pleasure to the new occupants. Being possibly a genuine lover of nature, the previous occupant did not follow a scorched earth policy with the rest of the garden too. The trees were all thus left behind and so were the few flowering and fruit-yielding bushes. None of the present residents had any idea about the names of the innumerable other flowers. In fact when some identical and strange looking objects appeared all over a bush, they thought that it was being affected by some pest. But in a couple of weeks, they were in for a pleasant surprise because these blossomed out into beautiful big red flowers. It was sheer ecstasy for Raghav and Radha to sit in this flowery paradise and watch the bees come and suck honey.

There were of course a number of birds too. A pair of minas in fact nested somewhere around the building. There were also pairs of cooing spotted doves all round. It gave Raghav quite a thrill to see a pair of parakeets land in their garden and suck honey from the flowers there. A few days later they saw an even more divine sight when a flock of cockatoos came and sat in the neighbour's garden. Two other species of birds, possibly flower-peckers and different types of minas, used to generally hover around the garden sucking honey from the flowers. It went without saying that the sights of these used to give Raghav, in particular, great joy. There were of course no magpie robins to be seen anywhere around, but there was a pair of magpies and their chick nesting in the neighborhood somewhere. One favorite perch of the magpies was on top of the electric pole which stood outside the entry to the house. A stage was soon reached when the birds nesting around would see him during his walks and cry out in recognition or to raise an alarm. Having never seen a magpie in India he went out of his way to show the bird to Radha and both agreed that the tweets of the bird were such that even their nightingale- Lata Mangeshkar – will have to bow her head in respect before the bird.

The locality in which they resided was not newly developed, but was in the outskirts of the city. Added to this was the fact that the density of population of the country was very low compared to that of India. Raghav would hence be looking at a totally desolate road when he stops his walk on the road outside in front of their house. But on most mornings at least one of the magpies would be perched on the pole and sing for a while with Raghav around.

It was hence a matter of pleasant surprise for Raghav to see a couple take a walk along the road outside the house, one morning. They entered a house in the neighbourhood, but, before doing so, it seemed to Raghav that they waved to him. Not to be left behind in social interaction, Raghav too waved back with gusto. He reported the incident with great pleasure to his relatives, but they found it hard to believe. They then even went on to suggest that the couple might have waved not to Raghav, but to someone else. Raghav was however not convinced. In fact, a couple of days later, he was on the verge of reaching near the pole outside the entry point of his house. He heard the magpies cry and looked up to have a better view. When he looked down again, he saw the same couple on their morning walk and waving to him again. He spontaneously waved back without any hesitation, giving also a warm smile. The magpie sang again.

24

Shunyavaad

(the belief that nothing in the world has a real existence)

Gopi believes that well begun is half-done. He therefore tries his best to see that his day starts off well. He does not have much choice in this regard, however. He is a married mortal and his wife Rema is often the very anti-thesis of his way of organized living. She insists on taking life as it comes. Not to talk of perspective planning, even planning for the very next day is not usually in her lexicon. Being an early bird, Gopi actually combines his ritual of a morning walk with shopping for fruits, vegetables and grocery to meet daily needs. Given a choice, he would actually like to plan this entire shopping the previous evening itself.

From the day Gopi surrendered his bachelordom, he has been left with little choice in this regard, however. Decisions regarding things to be bought are often postponed by Rema to the penultimate minute before the start of his morning routine. While in the beginning of his *grihastashrama* (Sanskrit word for the 25 year period in one's life between the ages of 25 and fifty during which one is supposed to focus mainly on household and business matters according to Hindu philosophy), this used to bug him considerably, he had become thick-skinned enough over time in this regard. With some difficulty, he ultimately succeeded in organizing a system by which at least a preliminary draft of the shopping list is got ready just before he sets out for his morning walk. But there would invariably be last-minute footnotes galore to this draft list that had got prepared. And, more often than not, these footnotes were much longer than the main text of the list.

Gopi was always known for counting his pennies. Add to this the fact that he had witnessed many a pick-pocketing incident in life. All this made him throw the baby out with the bathwater by being one of those who never carried a money purse. But since he was not a mobile phone savvy *paytm* guy, he had to perforce carry enough cash to pay for his morning shopping. This was all the more so because the public sector shops from where he got the things in the morning were yet to introduce facilities to accept card payments. Once the tentative shopping list was ready, his next task was therefore to decide on the amount of cash to be carried in his person for this purpose. Since he was a regular shopper from these shops with fixed and publicized prices, an estimate of expenditure to be incurred on this count could easily be made. To this, Gopi would add at the most 10% more to make allowance for unforeseen factors. This exact amount thus arrived at or its nearest equivalent would be taken out by Gopi from the kitty kept carefully and systematically for this purpose by Rema in her money-purse.

That November morning also, Gopi had gone through this entire rigmarole. He had bought vegetables worth Rs 183 and was waiting to collect the balance of Rs 17/-. To his surprise, the man at the counter was somehow starting to count a few five hundred and one hundred rupee notes too. He then went on to hand over a few of these to Gopi along with the Rs.17/-.

It took a few moments for Gopi to understand what was going on. On being asked, the shop-keeper explained that Gopi had actually given him a two thousand rupee note and not a two hundred rupee one. Being meticulously honest, Gopi simply declined to accept this extra money. The shopkeeper too refused to budge. There was thus a genuine difference of opinion.

It was found that the matter could be verified easily. This was so because Gopi was the very first customer. The shop-keeper examined the stock of notes that he had kept in his box for business purposes. He showed everyone around that the stock contained no two hundred rupee note at all. This clearly proved that he was right and Gopi, not quite so. Despite all this, it was with considerable hesitation that Gopi agreed to accept the entire amount supposedly due to him. In doing so, he took a deep look into the eyes of that shop-keeper to find childish innocence- so rare these days- writ large in them.

On returning home, he narrated the entire incident to Rema to be gently chided by her about his carelessness in mundane matters. The two then went on to examine the contents of the money purse to find that the shopkeeper was indeed right. There was only one two hundred rupee note in the purse and that was still there. Usually the two hundred rupee notes are kept along with the one hundred rupee notes in the purse. But due to some oversight, it was kept alongside two thousand rupee notes that day, possibly because both of them were more or less of the same color. Not surprising that Gopi, particularly poor at making finer distinctions between colors, did not also care to notice the third zero printed on it.

Or, maybe he thought it was just a *shunya* after all. The simple and mundane being that he was, he could simply not philosophize enough to find the concept between eternalism and nihilism. His heart was however beating fast with joy. The message that came through to him from this *shunya* (zero) event was crystal clear. So long as there were a few 'fools' like the shopkeeper still left on the face of Mother Earth, Gopi had no doubt that the Crack of Doom can be held in abeyance.

25

Why Not?

To make life easier, my working wife and I practice division of labor to run our home. The task of 'fruit and vegetable' shopping has fallen on my not so broad shoulders. I found this particular shopping task all the more onerous because I, neither enjoyed, nor was I particularly good at, bargaining and that too with vegetable and fruit vendors. Most of these Johnnies often find cheating me, mere child's play. Due to all this, I have devised my own means to make this unpleasant task less so. I go to the fixed price shop run by Mother Dairy to sell fruits and vegetables in my neighborhood for this purpose. Besides this price advantage, let me also state that some of the most interesting experiences that I have had in the recent past took place in this booth's precincts. I deem it proper to recount one such incident here particularly since it was a real eye-opener for me in terms of human attitudes and emotions.

It was 7 a.m. on a sultry morning in Delhi. The booth from where I buy fruits and vegetables had more than its usual share of customers that day. The group consisted predominantly of domestic helps of both sexes with lists in hand or in their minds and carrying over-sized bags. Then there were couples of different age-groups- the young DINKS, (double income no kids) the middle-aged *mia-biwis* (Husband-wife couples) and some real oldies. There were also individual shoppers of all ages and of both sexes doing their assigned jobs for their respective households. All this was so despite it being a working day on which people do not generally venture out early to make such purchases.

Over time therefore those who managed the booth found the sole counter in operation too crowded. They hence decided to open one more to disperse the crowd. Even this did not improve matters much. Queues started forming in front of both the counters. Soon there were at least five to six persons standing in a line at each of these counters with their shopping baskets overflowing with items waiting to be billed.

After going through this entire rigmarole, I was on the verge of leaving the booth when something near the exit caught my eye. Lying on the ground was a slightly crumpled five hundred rupee note. The booth was more than full of people. There were of course those standing in the two queues to collect and pay their bills at the conclusion of their shopping. Much larger in number were those still in the process of choosing their wares. There were also the few involved in the management of the booth. It was apparent that the note had fallen down from the hands of one of these persons inside the booth or from someone who had come to the booth and gone. Pondering over these possibilities, I deemed it proper to bend down and pick it up. Holding it high, I then went on to announce rather loudly that such a note was found near the exit of the booth.

All those, irrespective of age and gender, standing in the two lines, extended their hands to claim the note. So did almost all who were choosing their items. Those who were managing the booth were also not any way behind in staking their claim for the note. Without calling in expert detectives to decide the ownership of the note, I chose the easy way out. I simply handed it over to the management of the booth. After doing so, I suddenly remembered that I too had in my pocket a crumpled 500 rupee note. I had not checked whether it was still there or had fallen off. I did so post-haste and was much relieved to find that it was still there with me.

Goes without saying that one does not have to be a 'smart Alec'to agree that there will be very few who will let go of a free lunch.

26

Hawker's Travails

Pediatrics they say has a lot in common with geriatrics. It is pleasant to see the few parks in Delhi teem with children in the evenings. But crowd control is becoming a problem in Delhi's parks even in the mornings these days due to population aging. Oldies of all hues in demographic parlance - young old, old old and extremely old – manage to reach the park in the small hours of the morning and try, if possible to saunter, walk, brisk walk or even trot. Those who are not in a position to walk, just sit there for a couple of hours to catch a breath of fresh air and maybe to socialise a little. Since it is well-known that one should start watching one's figure even from the age of forty to continue to remain alive and kicking for years, there is also a smattering of slightly younger persons who form part of this crowd. Those with entrepreneurial sparks find this a wonderful business opportunity to sell their wares. As a result, while in the evenings it is the ice cream vendors who are found in large numbers near the gate of the park, in the mornings it is the turn of the vegetable vendor, fruit seller and sellers of tender coconuts to flock around. I pass by this park in the course of my morning walks and have noticed that there is at least one representative from each of these groups of vendors outside the gate of this park every morning doing brisk business.

Though I generally do not buy anything from these vendors, I have watched them in operation. After doing so, I must confess that I have a sneaking sympathy for them. It is generally accepted that with such street hawkers there is considerable flexibility about the prices. I have seen people in my neighborhood bargain like mad with them with a good deal of histrionics thrown in too. I did have a sex-bias earlier in this regard and was under the impression that women purchasers were generally the ones who struck harder bargains. But close observation of a large number of instances convinced me that this need not actually be so. If an award were to be given for being the bargainer par excellence, I would, with no hesitation, award it to Rajan a close relative of mine. He is a senior academic always neck-deep in research and other academic and administrative work having very little time to call his own. To avoid disturbance, he deliberately got a first floor flat allotted to him by the university, despite his wife having a vertigo problem. But come the call of the vegetable vendor Baburam in the morning from the road below, he would simply get metamorphosed. Snatching the bag for vegetables and some cash – invariably short and kept handy for this purpose- he would literally jump down for his welcome ritual.

Some ritual it was indeed! Baburam would be walking round these quarters pushing his bicycle on the carrier of which would be a big round basket with vegetables. After greeting each other somewhat effusively, the actual process takes off. Rajan first takes stock of the different types of vegetables that Baburam has brought. A discussion ensues for a few minutes between the two as to why other types of vegetables were not there in the basket. Rajan would insist on sample checking the quality of each type of vegetable brought irrespective of whether he has any intention of buying it or not. The quality check is done by visually examining it closely, smelling it and also by touching and pressing it. The last process of checking often leads to resistance by Baburam. At times there are even fierce quarrels on this count with Baburam often threatening to walk off if Rajan presses the vegetable or fruit so hard as to make it unsalable to anyone else. The threat acts as a deterrent and peace prevails at least temporarily. After another five minutes of dilly-dallying and general discussions about vegetables, Rajan zeroes in on the type and quantity of vegetables that he wants to purchase. He generally goes in for three or four different types of vegetables. There is some exploratory gunfire when Baburam starts using his own scale to weigh the vegetables. Rajan swears that Baburam's scale does not show the correct weight and insists that the weighing be done again with Rajan's weighing machine brought down by his domestic help for this purpose. More often than not, the difference in the weights shown by the two machines turn out to be so small as to be negligible.

All this is elementary compared to the nuclear holocaust that takes place at the time of the settlement about the amount to be paid. Baburam is as sharp in mental arithmetic as Rajan and the issue at stake is not the calculation of the amount, but the price to be charged. For each of the type of vegetable bought, Baburam would quote the price per unit justifying it on the basis of the weather, availability of supply, transportation problems etc. Invariably Rajan would try to slash it by at least 50% using the same arguments solidified on the basis of newspaper, radio and TV reports and also of information supposed to have been collected from other shops in the neighborhood. At what point exactly the deal is struck for each type of vegetable is a matter of chance. Rajan generally buys three to four varieties of vegetables from Baburam regularly. There are limits to patience even of poor street hawkers. In the case of Baburam, this is reached by the time Rajan starts his histrionics of going back upstairs without buying anything unless Baburam slashes the price of the last type of vegetable that Rajan was intending to buy. A tearful Baburam would simply fall at the feet of Rajan pleading *"Babuji, aap jo marzhi de do. Lekin, meri chuttikar do"* ("Sir, you pay me whatever you like. But, for God's sake, let me go). Rajan's would be one of the first houses in the university colony that Baburam would be visiting.

I therefore used to wonder why he should spoil his day by undergoing this ordeal first. Possibly he had a superstition that a *boni* (first cash payment received for the day) from Rajan would augur well for the rest of the day.

Baburam's experience with Rajan can even be considered as pleasant if one compares it with another incident. This happened before my own eyes to a street hawker of vegetables who generally positions himself outside the gate of our neighborhood park in the mornings. He is a thin and somewhat haggard-looking young man. Always soft-spoken, he has a smile for everyone. He manages to keep it on despite the bargaining onslaughts by the many that crowd round him. Among the regular visitors to the park, I have also been noticing three stocky men with somewhat unusual, but identical features. One of them looked slightly older than the other two. Maybe they were all three brothers or maybe one was the father and the other two, his sons. They seemed affluent because they came in their separate cars and were quite well dressed. Though they did participate in all the group activities in the park, they were not particularly friendly as they never returned the ready smile that I gave everyone I ran into. I have also been a witness to their behavior and could easily overhear the conversations that they have among themselves and with others. From these, I could easily make out that they were far from refined in their demeanor, with the usual four letter expletives of the north flowing freer than air during their regular parlance. Once I chanced to buy an item from this saintly looking vendor. I was on the verge of finalizing the deal, when in trooped these three musketeers. Without waiting for my deal to be completed, the person who reached the vendor first began pressing hard a watermelon that the vendor had, inviting a slightly disapproving glance from the vendor. This was possibly too much for the threesome and they decided to imbibe some home-truths to the vendor. Loudly stating that it was only by pressing hard that one could make out what was inside, one on them went very near the vendor. He then went on to press the right chest of the vendor hard and proclaimed to the rest of his gang in Hindi *'Auratonkeandarkyahaipatakarnekeliyeaisejhor se dabanapadtahai. Yeh dabanekecheezhai. Patahai?"* ("To find out what is inside a woman, one has to press hard like this. Do you know this is something to be pressed like this in women") All the three had a hearty laugh at this supposed joke. I did not somehow feel like joining in. I do not know whether the watermelon was ultimately purchased or not but I could certainly fathom the pang of helplessness, desperation and the seething undercurrent of rage in the eyes of the hapless vendor.

27

Poles Apart

If William Shakespeare were alive to-day, he would easily shout from the rooftops 'Extroversion personified, thy name is Raghavan Pillai'. Known more sans his caste tag, Raghavan's hall mark was his capacity to give an instant smile to all and sundry. This would dawn on his face even if a total stranger of any age or sex were just to wave to someone standing anywhere nearby, making him involuntarily respond with gusto. Further, Raghavan was more than adequately supplied with the gift of gab. This was so ample that anyone in conversation with him will feel not only at ease but even most cared for. Behind all this was the simple fact that his understanding of human nature was just profound. But even Raghavan had to bite the dust attempting to fathom the reason behind two of his recent experiences.

It was at a suburb of Melbourne that Raghavan first set his eyes on Ramesh. The two 'R's were in the city spending time with their respective NRI sons – Surendran and Gopal - whose families were friendly with each other. It was Raghavan's first visit to Surendran there, whereas Ramesh was in the habit of spending at least a few months every year with Gopal. Surendran and family, including visitor Raghavan, were invited to Ramesh's house for a formal meal in honor of Raghavan. This was reciprocated by Gopal. The opportunities for Ramesh and Raghavan to meet and interact were very many because the 'sons' were in the same exclusive social network with there being a dinner get-together at some place or the other every weekend. These frequent meetings strengthened their bonds even further. Ramesh started addressing Raghavan as *'Bhaisahib'* (A respectful form of address when talking to a slightly older male friend or member of the family.) since the latter was a shade elder to the former. A stage was soon reached when Ramesh would willingly attend a get-together only if he was assured that Bhaisahib would also be present there. The two families decided to drive from Melbourne to Sydney via Canberra. While there was considerable fun and even frolic for all during these trips, it was difficult to say whether it was the group of kids or the senior twain which enjoyed the most.

All good things they say come to an end and so were the visas of the two 'fathers'. By some curious coincidence they were ending on the very same day. Ramesh was returning to India a couple of days earlier and Raghavan, on the day before the visa expired. Around a week before their expected departure from Melbourne, the two met again at a function to celebrate the birthday of Gopal's daughter at a hired hall. It was a very well-attended function and Ramesh had his hands and feet full entertaining the guests many of whom flocked around him to wish him goodbye. It was with some difficulty that Raghavan succeeded in catching him alone. Quite keen to continue his friendship with Ramesh even after they both got back to Delhi, he requested Ramesh for his telephone number in Delhi. But surprisingly, he found Ramesh to be very hesitant to do so. Since Raghavan was not the one to take no for an answer easily, he just persevered. After a number of unsuccessful efforts, he found to his unpleasant surprise that for some strange reason, Ramesh was simply unwilling to oblige in this regard.

The human relations wizard – Raghavan - could just not make out as to where he went wrong to deserve this snub from his newly acquired pal - Ramesh.

The second incident when Raghavan was totally knocked out again was quite distinct from this first one in terms of both time and space.

Radha and Raghavan were spending time with their daughter Shalini and family at Ludhiana. They were put up at the beautifully planned Omega residential complex in the outskirts of the city. There is a club in the middle around which there is a well-planned park with basketball and tennis courts, and seats for people to sit and relax. Within a day of their arrival, Shalini took them to this spot. The couple fell in love with the ambience there and chose the venue for their regular evening jaunts. They could not help noticing that the city attracted people from different parts of India. Many of the laborers were from Bihar and one could also spot people from UP and Marwar, possibly running their businesses in this industrial hub of Punjab.

Raghavan had in his heart of hearts a slight built-in prejudice against businesspersons. It was not that he considered all business to be sinful. He did recognize that enterprise is the lifeblood of development. But he was also painfully aware of the unfair practices being indulged by many in business. It could also possibly be a case of grapes being sour. Even in his wildest dreams could he ever get the hang even of the simplest of 'businesses'. Nor was his experiences with Marwaris much to write home about. It was just confined to the neighborhood grocery store owner run by a person known for his uncouth demeanor and not so ethical business practices.

A couple of days after their arrival in Ludhiana, the Keralite pair was leaving the park in front of the club after their evening jaunt. At that same moment there entered the park another couple with a little child in a pram. The lady had the same sartorial preference like

Radha and was clad in a saree. She appeared to be the grandmother of the pram-borne little one. Her spouse was somewhat dark and looked around sixty. He was a little on the thin side with hardly any hair on his head. His moustache and whiskers had definite streaks of grey. Though he was far from being Mr. Handsome in appearance, he turned out to be the very last word in friendliness. The moment his eyes spotted Raghavan and his sari-clad wife, he gave the warmest of smiles to them. But Radha was more than surprised to find that the normally friendly Raghavan's smile in response was a very feeble one. This made Radha ask him later for this strange behavior of his. Raghavan confided in her that he did so because the couple looked every bit Marwari and he was not particularly keen on becoming friendly with members of that tribe.

What happened the next day was a near metamorphosis. The Kerala couple was at their jaunt when they heard someone speaking their mother tongue somewhere around. On looking around, they were surprised to find the 'Marwari couple' -sans their little grandchild-conversing with each other fluently in chaste Malayalam. This language warmth melted even the regionally prejudiced Raghavan. He willy-nilly decided to make friends with this Marwari couple who could converse in Malayalam. On exchanging notes further, it emerged that they- Raman and Devika-were not Marwaris at all. They actually belonged to Kerala and were spending time with their son and family working and hence residing in Ludhiana. To crown it all, Radha originally came from the same locality in Ernakulam as this couple. Hence the trio had many things in common to talk about, with Raghavan an interested listener.

The families of these two couples came closer over time. The route that Raghavan took on holidays for his ritual of a morning walk with his school-going grandson was the same as the one that Raman took for similar ritual with his son Siddharth, working for an Indian multinational. Raman introduced Siddharth to Raghavan and the two vibed well. Raman's daughter-in-law Seema occasionally walked with her in laws pushing her child in the pram in the evenings. She too got introduced to Raghavan and Radha.

Raghavan noticed something slightly unusual about Seema right from the beginning. For one, she was somewhat big built for a Malayali girl. Further what she said as soon as formal introductions were over was a little odd. She went out of her way to mention that she was not familiar with the language and was trying to learn it. This puzzled Raghavan a good deal. He began to wonder whether she was a non-Malayali. He soon set this doubt aside by recalling that many a Malayali brought up outside Kerala may not be familiar with Malayalam. The cat was out of the bag soon, however. The Punjabi girl Seema was a colleague of Siddharth and Cupid did the trick. Despite strong initial opposition from Siddharth's parents, the marriage was solemnised in Ernakulam.

The dormant romantic in Raghavan got aroused to its fullest height in coming to know of all this. Despite introvert Radha's feeble protests, he invited himself to Siddharth's residence in Ludhiana. He waxed eloquent there on the fact that the two grandchildren of Raman there will neither be Keralites nor Punjabis, but 100 per cent Indians instead. He would normally have expected Seema to be pleased as punch at these words of his. But for some strange reason, there was no such reaction whatsoever. Ignoring this cold-shouldering and trying to make Seema even more acceptable to her in-laws, he extended a warm and sincere invitation to Raman and family to come and say hello to him at his daughter's residence at a stone's throw from Siddharth's place. The return visit never took place despite Raghavan's repeated invitations.

Raghavan has yet to find a clear answer to this million dollar question too.

28

The End of the Beginning

I am no physicist. It is true that the mysteries of Science puzzle even laymen like me. But what intrigues me even more is the myriad of human emotions. The manner in which the innumerable dimensions of these evolve to make life what it is, has always made my heart beat faster. The four-dimensional continuum of space-time make for interesting studies of human emotions and the resultant interactions, leaving me at times dumb-struck.

Thanks to artificial intelligence, time travel is no more a dream. It did not surprise me one bit when I found my octogenarian self suddenly turned into a lad of nineteen the other day. Though a regular visitor to the gym, I could not be called well-built as my sixty-three inch frame was definitely on the short side. Further, in terms of complexion, I was much more like Krishna than like Rama. Despite that, Krishna's Gopi-chasing trait was never my hallmark, however. I was therefore fiercely jealous of my tall and thin friend Ramanathan Mahadevan who had come to study in India's capital despite being born and bred till then in the South. One reason for this was of course that he was heads and shoulders above me in height. Even more pinching was the fact that he had a way with girls that I did not have (but in my hearts I pined to have). To make matters worse he had both gift of the gab and also a flair for writing neither of which I had even in my dreams.

It was known among all including the girls that Mahadevan had come to Delhi to pursue a post-graduate course also to prepare better to achieve his dream of getting into the IAS (Indian Administrative Service). It was hence no wonder that he was the cynosure of many a girl. This was too much for me. I used to go out of my way to embarrass him for this relative strength of his.

I remember one incident in particular. Mahadevan was particularly close to one of the girls – Kakoli Dasgupta- doing another post-graduate course from the same institution. She was from one of the eastern provinces and her brother was also a student in the same institution. Possibly after meeting him and maybe to impress him even further, Kakoli also started preparing for the IAS and allied services examination. She was somewhat assertive in nature and the joke that I was mainly responsible for spreading was that while he was taking the IAS exam, she was opting for the IPS. The 11 'o'clock break was the ideal time for the different sets of students to meet, relax and socialize at least for a few minutes in the famous rendezvous of those days– the Uiversity coffee house. Running into Mahadevan in the coffee house one day, I mischievously asked him somewhat loudly "How is *khoki*?" Being somewhat of a gentleman, he did not give any reply, but blushed crimson and just disappeared from the scene. When he met me later he explained to me the reason for his behavior. At the time I tossed the question, the *khoki* Kakoli's brother was with him.

Time flew. Mahadevan could achieve his dream of getting into the IAS. His intellect, overall ability and accommodative nature made him not only soar high in the bureaucratic firmament and hold a very senior position, but also become the golden-eyed boy of the high and mighty in political power. His love life was also successful and he married Kakoli who became his homemaker rearing and bearing his children. I followed a totally different career -a teaching one – in which regular interaction with officialdom was not called for at all. So we never ran into each other till he had officially retired. By that time the ruling dispensation had changed making him fall out of favor and get under a cloud. I distinctly remember his tall frame making an appearance with his lady wife one particular day in the private residential colony where I resided.

A couple of days later we actually ran into each other. We exchanged greetings and on coming to know that I stayed in my own house in the same area, he made it a point to come to my doorstep. I extended an invitation to him to come in and have a cup of coffee with me, but he politely declined giving some flimsy excuse or the other. This made me wonder whether he had developed the stiff upper lip of his cadre which is a direct descendent of the British Civil Service. I also got a hunch that he was scouting for a house to purchase or stay and had come to have a *'dekho'* (Hindi word meaning a broad and cursory look) of my residence at least from outside.

A few years of slime floated down the Yamuna. I initially used to spot either Mahadevan or Kakoli or both of them together taking walks along the residential colony or shopping in the neighborhood market. This made me conjecture that they were put up in the same colony at a place quite near mine. But these spottings ceased and I stopped thinking about them. I too finally retired in the University parlance. Since I got some reconstruction done to my residence, I had to shift for some time to a house in the neighborhood in another block of the same colony. While going for the daily ritual of my morning walk from this temporary residence of mine, I was surprised to find a house nearby where the letter boxes had the names R.Mahadevan and Kakoli Dasgupta written on them. A couple of days later outside the same house with these letterboxes, I found the exact *humshakal* (Hindi word for look-alike) of Mahadevan. Standing next to him was a young lady in her early forties whose features were an amalgam of those of Mahadevan and Kakoli. But I was rushing somewhere that day. Further, I had a cap on making it hard, even for close friends used to seeing me every day, to make me out. I was hence not one bit surprised that Mahadevan showed no sign of recognition when I walked past him. But on the next day when I ran into him near his residence, the same thing happened again. This naturally set me thinking. This was so because this time I was not wearing my cap and I showed signs of recognition on my face. Somehow he seemed to ignore these and just chose to look straight through me.

This puzzled me beyond measure and hence the next time I came face to face with him, I chose to confront him. I simply asked him whether he was Ramanathan Mahadevan. He gave no answer though I was certain that he emerged from the house the letterbox of which contained his and his wife's names. I see him everyday start from the house with his letter-box, assemble in the neighborhood park for exercises for senior citizens and get back to his residence. Makes me wonder whether the amnesia that he has shown towards me is real or feigned?

Time refused to stand still and just forced me to retrace my steps to a decade back. I had just completed a detailed study of aging and was being asked to give talks on the topic. One such event was organized by the residents association in the neighborhood. It was to be chaired by a Mr.M.L.Kaul who was from the IAS. He had recently retired as the Secretary of a central ministry. It has to be admitted that there is in general a tendency to run down a person in power on the verge of retirement. This becomes all the more so if the political party in power during the person's tenure gets replaced by those who were in the opposition in the penultimate stages of a bureaucrat's retirement. An honest bureaucrat would of course always be at the receiving end of brickbats from both parties. A pliable 'yes' Minister will rule the roost by extending whole-hearted support to all the actions of the party in power. Mr. Kaul had done this and fortunately for him the party that he had extended bureaucratic support won the elections and continued to rule even at the time of his retirement. There were hence no witch hunts in terms of CBI enquiries or income-tax raids against him. On the contrary, he was being given due respect by the new government in view of his former official position. But internecine squabbles between bureaucrats and inter-ministerial turf war did result in some muck gathering round Mr. Kaul's image too.

Because of the passage of time and due to the prevalence of at least some semblance of a democratic process, the political group which ruled the country was different from that when Mr. Mahadevan was the Secretary. To make matters even worse, I was known for my sympathies with the group that was in power in Mr. Mahadevan's days. In view of all this, I was a little concerned about how the event will turn out. But in fairness to Mr. Kaul, he took my critical comments about government policies sportingly in his stride without throwing his bureaucratic weight around. We actually became somewhat friendly after the event. It emerged that we had both gone through the same educational institution for our undergraduate education despite the fact that these were done years apart. Exchanging notes further, we could decipher many a commonality between us in terms of our educational backgrounds, and even friends and acquaintances. Our friendship grew and he even suggested that I join the old students association of my undergraduate educational institution, which suggestion I politely declined for my own reasons. Mr. Kaul's health has also started declining for reasons also of age. There are indications of his short-term memory becoming less sharp than before. He has so far not stopped giving me the warm smile of recognition reserved for me. From what little I know of him, I do not think that he ever will. I cannot visualize his ever feigning amnesia to deliberately avoid me. And if he does get amnesia, his people will certainly not let him walk around alone in the neighborhood.

Makes me wonder whether there are indeed various kinds of amnesia? In any case, I am more than convinced now that it does take different kinds of people to make the world what it is.

29

Honesty Not Dead Yet

Rank rabid self-interest riding rough shod over finer values and emotions is making life increasingly difficult these days, particularly for the aged. As an octogenarian spending his silver years in Delhi, I experience this daily.

Possibly, the old adages that there is no fool like an old fool and that an old man and his money are easily parted have dug deep into the minds of the younger generation. As a result, whenever I buy something from a new shop, invariably they won't have the right change to return to me the correct balance. What is surprising is the fact this sort of behavior is meted out to me even by the shops that I regularly frequent. Further I have to be doubly vigilant about ensuring that the money given to me is still legal tender. On top of it all, people try to dump on me the most soiled, torn and patched up currency notes making it incumbent upon me to visit often a bank, located quite far away, where these notes are replaced by fresh ones. Talking of banks, I distinctly remember a young man with a sweet smile who tried to give me a couple of thousands less than what I had withdrawn thinking that I would not notice it.

On a particular morning, I was in a hectic hurry. I had to first visit a studio in the neighborhood market to collect copies of the photographs that I had got clicked there. Along with those photos, I had to rush to another office to fill up a form and submit it for some purpose. It was true that the studio was located at a distance at the most of two hundred metres from my residence. But I was already delayed and time was becoming more and more precious. I hence hired an auto-rickshaw for going to the studio and naturally reached there in a jiffy. To my disappointment, I found that I had forgotten to bring the slip on the receipt of which they will give me the photographs. So, I made the auto-rickshaw take me back home, wait for me to collect the slip and return once again to the studio. I got down, looked at the meter which showed a fare of Rs. 25/-. I took out a 50 Re note from my pocket and gave it to him asking him to take 30 Rs and return me Rs 20/-. My attention was somehow diverted for a brief moment making me turn my face in another direction. All the time, I was extending my open hand towards the auto-rickshaw driver expecting him to return me the balance. But no currency notes fell into my hand and so I turned back to find out what was happening. To my surprise, I found that there was no trace of the auto-rickshaw or its driver nearby. I looked a little further and found the vehicle being driven at great speed in a different direction.

My experiences with street vendors have also been equally unpleasant, if not more so. I often have to buy fruits from them and it is quite a nightmare to do so. I invariably find that the price quoted in my case is almost always a bit higher than that for the others. This makes me put on my bargaining cap and gently point out that there are shops where the thing can be got much cheaper. This cuts little ice and if I am perseverant, I am rudely told to buy it from that shop where according to me things are cheaper. There is an additional factor that makes matters worse in this regard. For reasons of age and health I am constrained to be somewhat particular about the quality of the fruits that I consume. My insistence in this regard leads to fierce resistance because often the attempt is to palm off to me at least a few rotten pieces along with rest. A real bad incident of this kind easily comes to my mind. I had gone to a market located slightly away from my residence. Fruit vendors abound there and I decided to buy a dozen oranges. The vendor I zeroed in volunteered to choose the oranges for me. But to his surprise, despite my age, I prevented him from doing so. When I started selecting only very good quality ones, I could see murder in his eyes. Coolly ignoring that, I also took care to see to it that he put them in a plastic bag and tied it up to be handed over to me after I made the payment. In the meantime a few more customers crowded round his pushcart. It took me a couple of minutes to take the right amount from my pocket and pay him. As soon as I did so, a tied plastic bag of oranges was given to me. I could easily make out that there were oranges inside and did not deem it necessary to check further. I went home with a sense of satiety. The anti-climax was when I untied the bag in the evening with the intention of eating a couple of good quality oranges. All the oranges inside were so rotten that they were unfit for human consumption. The clever hawker had switched the bag containing my chosen oranges for another one filled with terribly rotten ones. This was the last straw that made me develop a strong revulsion towards street hawkers.

But then there arise occasions when one just cannot do without their help. It was one of the national holidays in India when all establishments in the country had to remain closed. I suddenly realized that there were no biscuits at home to feed the two stray dogs that come to us regularly for their food. To meet the minimum requirements for the day in this regard, I needed at least three packets of marie biscuits. The only source from where I could get these would be from some hawker. I am aware that a number of hawkers usually hover around the milk booth in our neighborhood. I was not too sure whether they would be there on that day too. So, I waited for the newspaper vendor to come to find this out. In response to my query on this count, he assured me that a couple of hawkers were there at their usual places, despite it being a national holiday. I took the right amount of money – 30 Rs – to pay for the three packets that I intended to buy. To my surprise I also found that I had brand new notes with me maybe because I had got change for 100 Rs from the bank.

Fully armed, I thus darted off to the neighborhood milk booth on my mission. After reaching there I stopped by the first hawker that I came across and enquired whether he had marie biscuits. I was happy to find that his reply was in the affirmative. I then began wondering whether he will charge me a higher price particularly because of my advanced age, and he being a hawker with no shop being open. With some trepidation, I asked him the price per packet for these biscuits. I was greatly relieved to find that he was not charging a higher price. With a smile on my face, I went on to request him to give me three packets of these. As he was taking these out one by one, I began searching my pocket for the money that I had brought for this purpose. I was unpleasantly surprised to find that I had only two 10 Re notes with me. As a result, I was constrained to tell him to give me only two packets of biscuits and told him the reason also for this change in my order for biscuits. Though he was a little unhappy and even irritated at this, he agreed to comply with my request. He gave me my two packets and I gave him the money that I had taken for this purpose. With the transaction over, I was on the verge of returning to my residence when the vendor stopped me. He took out another packet of Marie biscuits and handed the packet over to me saying "*Bhaisahib*, what you gave me was 30 Rs and not twenty as you had thought. Your three ten rupee notes were so new and unsoiled that two of them almost stuck together making it appear that you were having only two such notes." I would never have known this, if the vendor had not tried to make amends in my favor for this oversight on my part.

After this incident, I am having second thoughts on my usual refrain that honesty is dead since long. I have also started wondering whether all can be tarred by the same brush.

"AUTHOR: K.R.G. Nair"